Joe felt a sudden shock of desire slam through him at the thought of what he'd really like to do with her this evening. He'd like to take her home and kiss her senseless. To strip that dress off her and run his hands over her body.

There was no reason why he shouldn't kiss her. Kissing was a normal part of dating, and this was supposed to be a date.

He hadn't spent so much time aroused since he'd been a teenager. And he was finding it a damned uncomfortable state to be in. At least when he knew that he couldn't follow his desires through to their logical end.

"I hadn't really thought that far ahead." He took refuge in a lie. "What would *you* like to do?"

Dear Reader,

I know you've all been anxiously awaiting the next book from Mary Lynn Baxter—so wait no more. Here it is, the MAN OF THE MONTH, *Tight-Fittin' Jeans*. Mary Lynn's books are known for their sexy heroes and sizzling sensuality…and this sure has both! Read and enjoy.

Every little girl dreams of marrying a handsome prince, but most women get to kiss a lot of toads before they find him. Read how three handsome princes find their very own princesses in Leanne Banks's delightful new miniseries HOW TO CATCH A PRINCESS. The fun begins this month with *The Five-Minute Bride*.

The other books this month are all so wonderful…you won't want to miss any of them! If you like humor, don't miss Maureen Child's *Have Bride, Need Groom*. For blazing drama, there's Sara Orwig's *A Baby for Mommy*. Susan Crosby's *Wedding Fever* provides a touch of dashing suspense. And Judith McWilliams's *Practice Husband* is warmly emotional.

There is something for everyone here at Desire! I hope you enjoy each and every one of these love stories.

Lucia Macro

Senior Editor

Please address questions and book requests to:
Silhouette Reader Service
U.S.: 3010 Walden Ave., P.O. Box 1325, Buffalo, NY 14269
Canadian: P.O. Box 609, Fort Erie, Ont. L2A 5X3

JUDITH McWILLIAMS
PRACTICE HUSBAND

SILHOUETTE *Desire*
Published by Silhouette Books
America's Publisher of Contemporary Romance

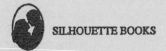

SILHOUETTE BOOKS

ISBN 0-373-76062-0

PRACTICE HUSBAND

Books by Judith McWilliams

Silhouette Desire

Reluctant Partners #441
A Perfect Season #545
That's My Baby #597
Anything's Possible! #911
The Man from Atlantis #954
Instant Husband #1001
Practice Husband #1062

Silhouette Romance

Gift of the Gods #479

JUDITH McWILLIAMS

began to enjoy romances while in search of the proverbial "happily ever afters." But she always found herself rewriting the endings, and eventually the beginnings, of the books she read. Then her husband finally suggested that she write novels of her own, and she's been doing so ever since. An ex-teacher with four children, Judith has traveled the country extensively with her husband and has been greatly influenced by those experiences. But while not tending the garden or caring for family, Judith does what she enjoys most: writing. She has also written under the name Charlotte Hines.

Prologue

"Much as it pains me to admit it, Adelaide Edson, you have absolutely no calling to become a nun."

Addy, well used to her aunt's habit of speaking her thoughts aloud, ignored the comment and finished giving the DPT inoculation to the screaming toddler on the examining table.

"He's in perfect health," Addy said as she handed him to his young mother. "Bring him back in six weeks for his second set of inoculations. Sooner, if you're worried about anything."

"Thank you, Miss Addy. Sister Margaret." The woman gave them a shy smile as she left.

Addy glanced around the empty tent in relief. "I was beginning to think we'd never get finished. I sure hope there's some iced tea left in the cafeteria, because I'm dying for a glass."

"What I want are a few answers," Sister Margaret said

as she helped Addy clean up the debris from the baby clinic.

Addy smiled affectionately at her. "Then why don't you try asking a few questions?"

To Addy's surprise, her aunt didn't smile back.

"This is no laughing matter, Addy. If you don't want to become a nun, what do you want out of life?"

"Aunt Margaret, I'm hot and tired and dirty and..."

"And avoiding my question," Sister Margaret finished. "I'm serious. It's long past time that you thought about it."

"I will, just as soon as—"

"Now." Sister Margaret's voice brooked no opposition, and Addy gave in. There was no point in arguing with her aunt when she was in this kind of mood. It was far easier to go along.

"What do I want out of life?" Addy repeated the question as she stared out through the open side of the tent at the small group of children who were playing in the scalding sun.

"Children," Addy tried the word out and then repeated it when it sounded good. "Children. I want to have some of my own. Three, maybe four."

Her aunt nodded. "That makes sense. One of the reasons you're such a good pediatric nurse is the empathy you have for children. But I should point out that in order to have children you first need to have sex and for that you need a man."

"Do tell." Addy grinned at the elderly woman.

"It's about time someone told you," Sister Margaret said tartly. "What's more, you're not likely to find a husband in a refugee camp in Western Africa run by nuns."

Addy felt her shoulders tense as the all-too-familiar feeling of inadequacy welled out of her subconscious. "I'm not likely to find one anywhere."

"Nonsense!" Sister Margaret said bracingly. "A lovely young woman like you?"

Addy blew a damp strand of dark red hair that had escaped from her functional chignon out of her face and looked down at her rumpled uniform, which was liberally stained with the results of treating scores of children.

"Your partiality is overwhelming your common sense," Addy muttered. "Besides, I may have spent the last four years in Africa, but if you remember, before that I was working in Chicago—a city with millions of men in it, and not a single one of them showed the slightest desire to marry me."

"And whose fault was that? You were always so defensive about being a little plump—"

"Fat," Addy corrected. "I wasn't plump. I was fat."

"Whatever!" Sister Margaret waved a dismissive hand. "The point is that you aren't overweight anymore. There's nothing to stop you from going out and grabbing a man to father those kids you want."

Addy suppressed a sigh. If all she wanted was a walking sperm bank, then maybe her aunt was right. But that wasn't all she wanted. She wanted more, a lot more. She wanted someone who was interested in her as a person as well as a sexual partner. She wanted someone to talk to, to share her hopes and fears with. To build a future with. A future that would last after their children had grown and left home.

Unfortunately, if she believed the letters she'd received over the years from her single girlfriends, men like that were scarcer than the proverbial hens' teeth.

And even if by some miracle she did run across a man who fit her requirements, it wouldn't do her any good. She wouldn't have the vaguest idea how to go about attracting his attention. And that was the crux of her problem. She squarely faced the fact. She didn't know. She didn't know how to attract men, how to talk to them, how to relate to them on any level. She had absolutely no experience to fall back on. As far as she was concerned, they might as well be another species entirely.

"Good, then we're decided." Sister Margaret chose to

take Addy's silence as agreement. "You're going to return home to Hamilton, find a husband and have some children to brighten my old age. Eastern Pennsylvania will be pretty, with fall coming," she offered as an added inducement.

A reluctant smile flickered in Addy's deep brown eyes. If only it were as easy as that. Of course, to her aunt, it probably was. Her aunt didn't seem prey to the self-doubts that had always haunted Addy.

"I'll make your plane reservations this afternoon."

Addy blinked. "This afternoon! What's the rush?"

"You aren't getting any younger, and if you wait for a good time to go, you'll never leave. This place is always in the middle of a crisis."

Sister Margaret turned to leave and then stopped, clicking her tongue in annoyance. "I almost forgot why I came over here in the first place. A letter came for you in the mailbag." She pulled a long white envelope out of her pocket and handed it to Addy.

Eagerly, Addy looked at the return address, hoping for a letter from a friend, and then grimaced.

"Bad news?" Sister Margaret asked.

"No, just old news. It's from that law firm that wants to buy the property that Mom and Dad's house sits on. Remember, I told you about their offer. They say they have a client that wants to build a factory or some such on it."

"Are you still adamant about not selling?"

"Yes. I grew up in that house, and even though Mom and Dad are both dead and I haven't lived there since I graduated from high school, I still think of it as home. And if I sell it, I won't belong anyplace." A feeling of panic swirled through Addy.

"All the more reason to get yourself a husband. People should belong to other people, not to a place," Sister Margaret said as she left.

I should be so lucky, Addy thought ruefully, wishing she had inherited even a tenth of her aunt's self-assurance.

She leaned back against the examining table and ripped

open the envelope, extracting the single sheet of paper. As she'd suspected, it was another offer to buy her property, virtually identical to the ones she'd been receiving for the past eighteen months. The only thing that changed was the price they were offering.

Addy frowned as she peered closer at the scrawled signature at the bottom of the page. No, one other thing had changed—the signature. Instead of being signed by a lawyer named Blandings as all the other ones had been, this letter was signed by the president of the company who wanted her land, one J. E. Barrington.

"J. E. Barrington," she muttered. Joseph Barrington? Could J. E. Barrington be her Joe Barrington? Not that Joe had ever been hers. In fact, when they were children, Joe hadn't appeared to belong to anyone. She couldn't remember ever seeing anyone attending a school function with him. Or standing on the sidelines during sporting events rooting for him. He'd always seemed to be alone, both physically and mentally.

But despite his aloofness, Joe had had a kinder side. A side Addy had discovered when she'd been in the second grade. She'd been standing on the playground after school crying because two boys from the fifth grade had taken her beloved doll and were beating its head on the pavement, saying that fat people didn't deserve dolls.

As if in answer to her tears, Joe had emerged from the school building and come to her rescue. He'd bloodied the nose of one of her tormentors, chased them both off and then told her that crying never helped anything. Only action solved problems.

After the incident, Joe had taken to walking her home after school, which had effectively ended the vicious teasing she'd endured. Not only that, but she'd acquired a friend. A prickly one, but the fact that he had never once referred to her being fat had made him absolutely perfect in her eyes. Their friendship had lasted until he'd gone away to college and they'd lost touch.

She glanced back down at the signature. Could it be Joe? Had Joe managed to build up a company from nothing? It was certainly possible, she conceded. If ever there was a person who had the will to succeed, it was Joe.

Thoughtfully, she shoved the letter into her pocket. Instead of writing a reply turning down their offer as she usually did, she would go to see this J. E. Barrington in person when she got back to Hamilton, she decided. It would be interesting to find out exactly who he was.

One

"**P**rogress rears its ugly head," Addy muttered as she pulled into the parking lot of the company that was so determined to acquire her land. When she'd been in high school the whole area had been gently rolling pastureland.

Addy cut the engine of her new compact, which she'd picked up from the dealer that morning, and studied the ultramodern building for a long moment. Now that she was actually here, she was of two minds about going in.

She had very fond memories of Joe. In fact, the only fond memories of the entire male sex she had from school were of Joe. If he had turned into a ruthless, money-grubbing businessman, she wasn't sure she wanted to know.

Aware that she was being ridiculous, Addy unbuckled her seat belt and got out. Whatever Joe had become had nothing to do with her. She had enough problems of her own to worry about. Such as how she was going to find a man to build a relationship with.

Addy checked the front of her cream linen suit to make sure it was still spotless, hooked her brown leather purse over her shoulder and headed for the oversized double doors at the front of the building.

Pushing one door open, she stepped inside and glanced around curiously. There was a gorgeously dressed, perfectly made-up blonde sitting behind a reception desk, who made Addy suddenly feel dowdy.

The blonde gave her a practiced smile and asked, "May I help you?"

"Yes, thank you. I'd like to see Mr. J. E. Barrington."

The blonde's perfectly curved eyebrows lifted as if to say, "Who wouldn't?" and asked, "You have an appointment?"

"No," Addy admitted, "but since he's been trying to buy my property for the past eighteen months, I assumed he'd be willing to see me if I stopped by."

"I'll check." The blonde suddenly became brisk at the mention of the property. "What name should I give him?"

Addy beat down a childish impulse to say "Queen Victoria" and dutifully gave her own name.

The blonde picked up the phone, held a brief conversation with someone at the other end and then said, "Mr. Barrington can spare you a few minutes. Just go through there." She pointed toward the door to her right. "Mr. Barrington's office is at the end of the hall."

"Thank you." Addy smiled at the woman and, clutching her purse like a lifeline, headed down the hall. Despite her curiosity about Joe, she wasn't looking forward to this interview. Whoever J. E. Barrington turned out to be, he still wanted her property and she still wasn't going to give it to him. He'd probably get insistent, and when that didn't work, he could well get sarcastic, and she hated dealing with sarcasm. It made her feel ten years old again. Overweight and unlovely and somehow not quite as good as everyone else. Almost as if she didn't have the right to say no.

But you aren't ten years old. You're a very competent thirty-two. And you aren't fat anymore either, she reminded herself, something that she found herself doing on an almost daily basis because, despite what her mind told her and her mirror showed her, she still felt fat on the inside.

At the end of the short hallway, Addy found herself in a reception area filled with comfortable leather chairs. Several doors led from it to what Addy assumed were offices. As she watched, one of them opened and a man in his late thirties wearing a well-cut black suit and a very conservatively striped tie hurried toward her.

"You must be Miss Edson?"

Not her Joe. Addy felt a flash of disappointment, the strength of which caught her by surprise.

"Yes, and you're Mr. Barrington?"

The man smiled self-deprecatingly. "No, no. I'm Bill Bernette, Mr. Barrington's executive assistant. Mr. Barrington's office is through here."

He lead her across the room. Knocking perfunctorily on the heavy oak door, he opened it and gestured Addy inside. "Mr. Barrington will be with you as soon as he finishes his call," he whispered, motioning her toward a seat in front of the desk.

Addy sank down in the chair and glanced curiously at the man on the phone. A feeling of disorientation hit her as she recognized his face. It *was* her Joe! Her eyes swept over his short, inky-black hair, then skittered across the tiny scar high on his left cheekbone to land in the sparkling depths of his deep blue eyes.

She felt as if she'd suddenly been transported back in time at a dizzying speed, leaving her stomach behind. She watched as he nodded at her, his lips shaping a brief, impersonal smile. Didn't he remember her? To her surprise, the idea hurt.

She remembered him. Her eyes focused on his mouth, tracing the firm contours of the dusky pink flesh. A shiver chased over her at the thought of pressing her lips against his. Of feeling them moving against hers. Of... Addy jerked her gaze away in a vain attempt to control her uncharacteristic thoughts. She watched as his hand impatiently tapped out a rhythm on the highly polished mahogany of his desktop. His long fingers were lightly tanned and the nails immaculately clean. She automatically looked for a wedding band, but didn't find one.

Because Joe wasn't married, or because he didn't wear one? Addy felt a shimmer of uneasiness at her curiosity. Her intense reaction to him wasn't like her, and it worried her. Jet lag, she told herself, dredging up the first excuse that came to mind and trying hard to believe it.

"Good God!" The exclamation cut through her thoughts and she glanced up, to find her gaze snared by the glittering sparks in his eyes.

"Addy? Is that really you?"

Addy winced at his incredulous tone. "Did I look that bad that you don't believe the improvement?"

"Improvement?"

She stated the obvious. "I'm not fat anymore."

He took her comment as an invitation to look at her, and Addy felt her skin tighten as his hot, blue gaze slowly wandered over her. She could feel her breasts tightening as his gaze lingered on them.

"No," he agreed, "you're not fat anymore." His eyes narrowed. "In fact, you look downright skinny. What have you been doing to yourself?"

Addy blinked at his description. No one had ever called her skinny in her life. It wasn't an idea she could relate to, so she ignored it.

"I've spent the last four years with a bunch of nuns trying to save the world," she said self-mockingly.

"From what I've seen of the world, you're lucky to still be in one piece. The world generally takes exception to being saved."

"Not my part of it. I work with children, and they're

darlings no matter where you find them." Her voice unconsciously softened.

"Teacher?" he guessed.

Addy felt a stab of disappointment that he didn't know. A feeling that she told herself was ridiculous. She was nothing more than an old school friend. There was no reason why he should have kept up with her life. She hadn't kept up with his.

"I'm a pediatric nurse-practitioner."

"As well as the owner of a parcel of land that we need."

His reference to her land brought Addy back to reality with a thump.

"We really need that land, Addy."

"*You* really need that land," she corrected. "I already have it, and I intend to keep it."

Addy watched as his eyes narrowed, showing a line of fine wrinkles at the corners. As if he laughed a lot. Her gaze dropped to the firm set of his jaw, and she mentally rejected the idea. He probably just spent a lot of time outside in the sunlight.

"Addy, be reasonable." His plaintive words echoed through her mind, dislodging old memories. He must have said those exact same words to her hundreds of times when they were children. The familiar sound of them served to dispel the strangeness of her reaction to him. Suddenly, he was simply Joe. Her childhood friend.

She grinned at him, inexplicably feeling carefree. "If memory serves me right, your idea of being reasonable means that I do exactly what you want."

Joe shrugged, and Addy watched in fascination as his powerful shoulders moved beneath the perfection of his custom-tailored suit. In some strange way, his highly civilized clothes didn't make him seem civilized. They actually seemed to make him more ruggedly masculine, as if their purpose was to highlight the difference between the way he really was and the way he wanted people to perceive him.

"I really need that land, Addy," he said. "Our present plant has reached capacity, and we need to expand to meet the increasing demand."

"Demand for what?" Addy asked, curious about what he did.

"Computer chips."

"Oh," Addy said, "You're one of *them*."

"One of who?"

"One of those fanatics who want to put computers everywhere. Do you know they're even putting the blasted things in libraries?" she said in remembered outrage. "They're getting rid of card catalogues and making you use computers, and half the time they don't even work."

Joe grinned at her, giving her a glimpse of his gleaming, white teeth. "You may look a lot different, but you haven't really changed. You can still divert a conversation quicker than anyone I know."

Addy felt her spirits rise at the warmth of his smile. A smile that was echoed by the sparkle of humor in his eyes.

"But the fact remains that I need your land."

"I know you want it, but I want it, too. It's..." Addy struggled to explain her feelings. "That house is all I have left of my folks. I grew up there. All my memories are there. If I sell it and you raze it, they'll all be gone."

"Your memories aren't in the house, they're in your mind. And nothing I or anyone else can ever do will destroy them. Be grateful you've got happy memories to cherish."

His voice took on a bitter tinge, and Addy suddenly remembered overhearing her mother and her friends whispering about the disgraceful way Joe's mother drank.

"Why don't you simply build your plant somewhere else?" Addy ventured. "I can't own the only vacant tract in town."

"Yours is the best," he insisted. "The location is perfect. Every other site that's available had big problems. Our engineers—"

Joe paused as his assistant stuck his head in the door and

said, "You asked me to tell you when Hodkins over at the bank called. He's on the line now."

"Addy, would you mind waiting a minute while I take this call?" Joe asked as he reached for his phone. "It's important."

Deciding to take advantage of the interruption, Addy got to her feet. She needed to think about what Joe had said and she found it hard to do it when he was just a few feet from her. Somehow, the sight of him did strange things to her thought processes.

"Of course not, Joe. I promised a friend I'd drop by this morning, and it's almost noon now."

"But we haven't reached an agreement."

"I'll give you a call this afternoon," Addy said and then escaped. She had the feeling that people didn't reach an agreement with Joe. They gave in to him. The very forcefulness of his personality would tend to wear down the opposition.

She gave the surprised-looking Bill a quick smile as she hurried down the hall, breathing a sigh of relief when she was out of the building. Kathy should be able to tell her all about Joe. Addy unconsciously sped up at the thought. Kathy had always known all the gossip when they were in school together.

"Addy!" Joe stuck his head out of his office and glanced around the deserted reception area.

"She went that-a-way." Bill gestured toward the exit. "Would you like me to see if I can catch her?"

"Fat chance you'd have of getting her to do anything she didn't want to. She was always the most aggravating, stubborn kid...."

Bill stared thoughtfully in the direction Addy had gone. "I don't know about that, but she sure turned out spectacularly."

A shaft of anger lanced through Joe at Bill's bemused expression.

"Leave her alone!" Joe's harsh command surprised

them both. He hadn't meant to say it. He'd thought it, but he hadn't meant to say it.

"I'm trying to negotiate with her for her land," Joe added, to rationalize his order. "I don't need any complications from you chasing her."

"It's only a complication if I catch her." Bill chuckled and then hastily sobered at Joe's scowl.

Bill held up his hand in a gesture of surrender. "Sorry. I won't make one move until after you've finished the negotiations. What about your phone call?"

"Dammit! I left him hanging when she bolted." Joe hurried over to the phone. Addy was still the most aggravating woman he'd ever met.

"Barrington here," he said.

"Good morning, Mr. Barrington. This is Sean Hodkins. You asked me to let you know when the bank reached a decision on the loan David Edwards applied for?"

You mean I bribed you to let me know, Joe thought cynically. "I take it you have news?"

"Yes, the bank turned him down. The loan committee felt that his company was already badly overextended, and that young Mr. Edwards didn't have a viable plan for turning his family's company around."

Joe bit down on the sense of exultation that filled him. At long last, after years of waiting and planning, he was finally going to be able to exact revenge on the Edwards family for what they had done.

"You did as I asked?" Joe kept his voice level with an effort.

"Yes, sir. Exactly as you said. When Mr. Edwards came out, I offered him your business card and told him that your company was looking to invest excess profits and preferred to do it locally. I suggested he contact you."

"What did he say?"

"He said he was glad someone was able to make a profit in business because he sure didn't seem to have the knack."

"Did he take the card?" Joe demanded.

"Yes, although he didn't look at it. He just stuffed it into his pocket. Poor man, I'm afraid the committee's rejection was a real blow to him."

If so, it was one of the few blows that had ever landed in David Edwards's charmed life, Joe thought grimly. But that was about to change. He was about to experience how the rest of the world lived.

"Wait until tomorrow and then give him a call and remind him of what you said," Joe ordered. "By then he should be more receptive to the idea."

"Oh, I will," Hodkins said earnestly. "It would be a shame if the Edwards Corporation were to fold. Why, that plant's been here since my great-grandfather's time. And young Mr. Edwards seems like such a nice man."

"Give me a call if you hear anything else." Joe cut him off. He didn't want to hear David Edwards's praises sung. He knew better.

Joe hung up the phone and leaned back in his chair as a sense of satisfaction filled him. It had taken him his entire life to reach this point, but he was finally here. Within months, sooner if he were lucky, the Edwards Corporation would belong to him. His mouth tightened. As it should have all along.

And with Addy's land... An unconscious smile curved his lips as he thought of her. Who would have ever thought that she would turn out as she had? Once in a while over the years he'd caught sight of a redhead in a crowd and he'd thought of her, wondering where she was and what she was doing. But never in his wildest flights of imagination had he ever thought that she'd look so infinitely alluring.

What would it be like to take her in his arms? he wondered. To kiss the soft lusciousness of her full mouth. To nuzzle her neck and to cup the weight of her breast in his hand. To...

No! With a monumental effort, he clamped down on the erotic images his mind insisted on playing. Addy was strictly out of bounds, he told himself. Anyone who had spent the last four years of her life helping out a group of nuns was not the type of woman who would be interested in an affair.

Addy was the type who would expect a declaration of undying love, followed by a marriage proposal. Something he had no intention of offering, because no matter how wild the sex was in the beginning, it invariably cooled, leaving a man trapped in a stale, boring relationship.

Far better to keep Addy as a friend. And she was his friend. The thought brought a feeling of pleasure in its wake. They might not have seen each other in years, but they shared a history that went back to grade school. Not only was she his friend, but he trusted her. In fact, she was one of the few people in the world that he did trust.

No, he repeated, Addy was his friend and sex would screw that up. Sex was easy to come by if that was all a man wanted. Friends were a lot more precious. He reached for the pile of papers he'd been working on with a feeling of anticipation that hadn't been there before Addy's reentry into his life.

"Addy?" A short woman in her early thirties peered out through her screen door. "Is that really you?"

Addy chuckled at Kathy's incredulous tone. "Yes, so open the door and let me in."

Kathy hurriedly shoved open the screen. "Sorry, I was kind of... How on earth did you lose all that weight?" she blurted out.

"It just kind of happened," Addy said, as disconcerted by the sight of Kathy as her friend apparently was by her. Kathy had always been impeccably turned out in an appropriate outfit, whatever the occasion. Yet now she was wearing a pair of jeans that were frayed around the legs and a sweatshirt that looked as if it had been caught in the middle of a food fight.

Curious, Addy followed Kathy through the littered hallway into a bright, sunny kitchen. The source of the food splotches on Kathy's clothes was immediately apparent. A toddler was sitting in a high chair, happily smearing what looked like applesauce into his brown hair.

Addy chuckled at his beatific expression. "That, I take it, is Jimmy?"

"The one and only, and don't encourage him. His father already spoils him rotten. Have a seat." Kathy shoved a pile of dirty laundry off a chair onto the floor.

Addy sat down.

"When did you get back?" Kathy demanded.

"Last night. Hi, Jimmy." Addy smiled at the little boy. To her delight, he smiled back and tossed her a spoonful of applesauce. Fortunately, his aim wasn't very good and it hit the table instead.

"You always did have a way with kids," Kathy said. "Remember when our mothers would volunteer us to baby-sit in the church nursery? You could always get the screamers to shut up. Want some coffee?"

"No, I want some information."

Kathy ducked as Jimmy again flung applesauce in her direction. "How about motherhood isn't all it's cracked up to be?"

Addy laughed. "Few things are."

"Marriage is." Kathy's face took on a dreamy cast. "Jim is a fantastic husband. Now that you're home, we've got to find you one."

"I'm willing to consider any and all offers."

Kathy blinked. "What?"

"I said that I would like to get married, and I'm willing to consider all options."

Kathy stared at Addy in suspicion. "Are you making fun of my matchmaking tendencies?"

"No, I'm hoping to use them. I'd like to have some kids of my own."

Kathy glanced around the disheveled kitchen and shuddered. "On your head be it. How can I help?"

"Do you know any eligible bachelors?"

Kathy pursed her lips thoughtfully. "Let's see. There's Bart Dandridge, but I think we'd best stay away from him."

"Why?" Addy asked curiously.

"One of the partners in Jim's law firm handled his divorce and, according to him, Bart's wife claimed he beat her up a couple of times. I don't know if it's true or not, but…"

"I'll pass on Bart," Addy agreed.

"There's Tom, who's a bachelor friend of Jim's," Kathy said slowly. "He's pretty nice, but he does tend to drink a little too much. Jim had to represent him in a drunk-driving charge last month."

"Forget Tom. I don't expect perfection in a husband, but I do want sobriety."

Kathy sighed. "Addy, you've left it till very late. The good ones have long since been snapped up. Although…" Kathy's admiring gaze ran down the length of Addy's trim figure. "You look a lot better than any wife I know. Including myself."

"Thanks," Addy muttered, squelching her instinctive urge to make a self-deprecating response.

"Tell you what, I'll ask Jim when he gets home from work tonight. Maybe he can think of someone I can introduce you to."

Jimmy suddenly tossed his bowl on the floor and started to howl.

"Be quiet, brat." Kathy's loving tone belied her words as she took a wet cloth and scrubbed the applesauce off him. When he was reasonably clean, she set him on the floor and turned back to Addy.

"It might help if I knew what you are looking for in a husband."

Addy blinked as an image of Joe's features floated through her mind. No. She purposefully banished them. Joe was not husband material. At least, not for someone as inexperienced as she was. She ignored the irrational sense of loss that filled her.

"Well… He has to be willing to work and to like kids and to be clean. And a nonsmoker."

"You forgot a good lover," Kathy said. "Believe me, great sex can cover a multitude of other deficiencies."

What kind of lover would Joe be? Addy wondered, and then flushed when she realized where her thoughts were headed.

"I wouldn't know," Addy said primly.

Kathy stared at her friend in shock. "Don't tell me you're still a virgin!"

"I'm never going to tell you anything about my sex life, because it's none of your business."

Kathy chuckled. "Ah, hit a nerve there, did I? Tell me, do you still know anyone from around here?"

"Just Joe."

Kathy frowned. "Joe? Joe who?"

"Joe Barrington."

Kathy's mouth dropped open. "*Just Joe!* Are you out of your tiny little mind, woman? That man isn't *just* anything. How on earth did you ever meet the town's most eligible bachelor?"

"Is he?" Addy asked curiously.

"Is he what?"

"A bachelor?"

"Yup. No woman has ever managed to tie him down. And believe me, it hasn't been for lack of trying. Now, spill it. How did you meet him?"

"He rescued my favorite doll."

"What?"

Addy laughed at Kathy's confused expression. "I was in the second grade, and he must have been in about the fifth. It seems like I've known him forever."

"Yeah, but that was then. This is now. Now, he moves in entirely different economic circles from the likes of you and me. His last girlfriend was some model who was regularly decorating the pages of *Vogue*."

"What's his present girlfriend do?" Addy tried to make the question sound casual.

Kathy shrugged. "According to local gossip he hasn't replaced her yet. Of course I can't guarantee it. Joe is not a man who socializes much. In fact, he doesn't socialize with anyone around here at all. You might find that he doesn't even remember who you are."

"He remembered." Addy felt a great deal of satisfaction at the words.

"You've seen him already?" Kathy asked avidly.

"That's where I just came from. His company wants to buy my parents' property."

"Oh, so that's it. I heard talk that he might be planning to expand. Are you going to sell to him, Addy?" Kathy suddenly looked serious. "The town could sure use the jobs. Too many young couples have to move away because there's no work for them here. I..." she broke off as Jimmy toddled back into the room holding a can of soda that he was dribbling down the front of him.

"Blast his father!" Kathy muttered. "If I've told Jim once, I've told him a hundred times, not to leave half-empty cans of soda sitting around. Now I'll have to give the little monster a bath."

Addy got to her feet. "I'll leave you to it."

"You don't have to go," Kathy said. "It won't take me long."

"Thanks, but I still need to check with the realty company that handled the lease on the house for me while I was gone. I just wanted to touch base with you first."

Kathy gave her a warm smile. "I'm glad you did, and I'm even more glad that you're thinking about marrying and staying this time. I'll give you a call later."

"Thanks." Addy picked up her purse and let herself out.

With a last wave at Kathy, Addy climbed into her car and headed toward the realty office, her mind full of what

Kathy had said. So Joe was a bachelor, apparently one of the very few around. A sense of discouragement filled her, but she refused to allow it to grow. She'd known from the first that her goal wouldn't be easily reached.

Addy pulled into the turn lane and waited for the traffic to clear.

If only she had a little more experience at interacting socially with men. But wishing couldn't change the facts. Her mirror might tell her that she was slender, but in her mind she still felt fat. Fat and unattractive. When a man tried to make small talk with her, she froze. She mumbled awkward comments at random and the man invariably drifted away to find someone easier to talk to.

But how was she supposed to go about getting experience talking to men? she wondered in despair. Most women learned the skill in junior high school. She turned left as the light changed.

What she really needed was a brother who could give her good advice on what men liked and didn't like. But she didn't have a brother. Or even a cousin. But there was Joe, she thought, as the memory of his championship of her during their school years came to mind. He had been very kind to her back then. But was he still kind? Kindness and big business seemed an unlikely combination.

Besides, he was a very busy man. That much had been obvious from her brief visit this morning. Why should he take the time to help her learn how to relate to men?

Because he wanted to buy her property! The need wasn't all on her side. Joe wanted something too. He wanted her land and, while she really didn't want to sell, Kathy was right. It was selfish of her to hang on to the past when so many people could benefit by her letting go.

She could offer to sell him the house if he would help her learn the skills necessary to get a husband. If Joe agreed... A surge of excitement filled her. It was certainly worth a try. After all, the worst thing that could happen would be that he'd say no.

Two

"**D**o you have a reservation, sir?" The hostess eyed Joe as if he were a particularly appetizing entrée.

"Yes. Barrington." Joe glanced around the crowded restaurant looking for Addy, oblivious of the hostess's interest. "I'm meeting a Miss Edson."

"She hasn't arrived yet." The hostess became business-like at the mention of another woman. "Should I show you to your table now or would you prefer to wait in the bar?"

"The table, please." Joe followed the woman through the busy restaurant to a secluded table for two in one corner.

"Thank you." Joe sat down facing the doorway and checked his watch. Addy had said she'd meet him here at eight, and it was just after that now. So where was she? Could she have changed her mind? He certainly hoped not. He needed her property, and he needed it now. But then his need had never been in question. Only her willingness to sell.

So what inducement could he offer her to part with it? He didn't have a clue. Everyone else he knew responded to money. Offer them enough cash, and they caved in and did exactly what you wanted.

But Addy didn't fit the normal mold. Money didn't appear to hold the slightest fascination for her. According to what Hodkins over at the bank had told him, she hadn't even touched the substantial amount that her parents had left her. Not even the interest on it. And her rushing off to Africa to do good works was further proof that she simply wasn't motivated by conventional things. The women he knew were totally preoccupied with their own interests, not those of starving kids half a world away. No, Addy was definitely different.

He absently drummed his fingers on the pristine white tablecloth as he considered the situation. But that didn't mean that there wasn't something that she wanted. It simply meant that it would be harder to figure out.

Unconsciously, his lips lifted in a reminiscent smile as the memory of her clutching a doll to her pudgy chest and smiling at him through her tears when he'd routed her tormentors all those years ago flickered through his mind. Poor Addy. She may have had loving parents, but in a lot of respects her childhood hadn't been much happier than his.

She'd borne the brunt of her peers' teasing because her body hadn't conformed to what society said it should, while he'd been tarnished by his mother's drinking. Not that it was his mother's fault. Joe's features momentarily hardened. It had been her lover's fault. But the day of reckoning was coming, he promised himself. Very soon.

His eyes narrowed as a redheaded woman entered the restaurant, and Joe felt a curious sense of pride twist through him when he recognized Addy. Pride that Addy had turned out so well. So very well. The silky, emerald material of her dress clung lovingly to her slender curves, hinting at what it covered. His eyes lingered on the tantalizing swell of her breasts.

It was strange that she could look so overwhelmingly sexy without really revealing anything. Her neckline didn't expose her breasts, nor was her skirt short. And yet, despite the lack of specifics, he could feel himself getting hard just looking at her.

With a monumental effort, he blocked out his response as he got to his feet. Addy was a friend, he reminded himself.

Addy felt herself tense as she noticed Joe's expression. Was he annoyed that she'd asked him to meet her here for dinner? Had he had other plans that her request had interfered with? Such as a previous date? But if that had been the case, he probably would have said so, she decided. Joe had never been the least bit reticent about saying what he thought before.

"Good evening, Addy." He held a chair for her, and she sank down into it.

"May I get you a drink?" the waitress offered.

"Addy?" Joe asked.

"A glass of iced tea," she said, wanting to keep her wits about her. She was nervous enough about what she was going to ask Joe. It wouldn't help anything if she were to muddle up her thoughts with alcohol.

Joe's dark eyebrows shot up at her choice, but to her relief he didn't say anything. He merely ordered Scotch and water.

When the waitress left, he turned to Addy and said, "The message you left said that you wanted to discuss my offer?"

Addy gave him a rueful grin. Whoever had said that nothing ever changed must have had Joe in mind. He was exactly the same as he always had been. No small talk. Just go right to the heart of the matter. Would he make love like that? The unexpected thought popped full-blown into her mind. Would he be a physical lover without spending a lot of time on talk? Would he...

Stop it! She hauled her imagination up short. It was no business of hers what kind of lover Joe was. And she didn't want it to be, she assured herself. She had no desire to engage in casual sex and, while she was certain that sex with Joe wouldn't be the least bit casual, it would be a disaster. At least for her. She hadn't really needed Kathy to tell her that Joe was not a man who was interested in marriage. It was written all over him. Even someone as inexperienced as she was could tell that. Business was Joe's love. A woman would come in a poor second.

"Here you are." The cheerful voice of the waitress as she delivered their drinks interrupted Addy's thoughts, and she let them fade away.

"Well, you were saying?" Joe persisted when the waitress left.

"I wasn't saying anything. You were demanding."

"You were the one who asked me to meet you here. Why?"

Addy took a deep breath and mentally scrambled to marshal her thoughts. She was pretty certain that his first reaction was going to be negative. Nervously, she studied the firm line of his clean-shaven jaw. Very negative. Which was why she had asked him to meet her here. She'd figured that no matter how negative Joe felt about her proposal, he wouldn't yell at her in a public place. Nor was he likely to get up and leave. Here, she at least had a chance of getting him to consider her proposal seriously instead of automatically rejecting it.

Joe studied the curious play of emotions flitting across her face. She was very nervous about something, which probably meant that he should be nervous, too.

"Just spit it out," he ordered.

"It isn't that simple."

"Negotiations rarely are. But we're never going to get

anywhere if you can't bring yourself to make me a counteroffer.''

''I need to explain something to you first.'' Addy groped for words, wanting him to understand what she felt in the hope that he'd be more sympathetic to what she wanted.

Joe took a long swallow of his Scotch, studying her over the rim of the glass. ''About what?'' he finally asked.

''About why I came back from Africa. You see, my Aunt Margaret asked me if I wanted to be a nun.''

A nun! No! His mind totally repudiated the idea. Not his Addy.

Addy chuckled at his expression. ''That was kind of my reaction, too. Not that there's anything wrong with being a nun, it's just that it isn't right for me.''

Joe felt some of his tenseness dissolve at her reassuring words.

''But the question did make me examine what it was that I wanted to do with my life,'' Addy continued. ''Something I've never done before. I've simply sort of gone with the flow.''

''Like most people,'' he said cautiously, wondering where this was leading.

''Yes.'' She nodded in agreement. ''Anyway, when I thought about it, I realized that it wasn't really a *what* I wanted so much as a *who*. Or several whos.''

Addy leaned forward in her eagerness to explain, and Joe's eyes were drawn to the neckline of her dress, which at that angle was giving him a tantalizing glimpse of the swell of her breasts. He swallowed and forced his eyes up to her earnest face.

''What whos?'' he asked.

''A husband and kids,'' she blurted out.

Joe's eyes widened as the impact of what she was saying hit him with the force of a blow. She couldn't mean that she wanted him to marry her, could she? A confusing swirl of emotions tore through him, the overriding one being panic.

"But I have a problem," she continued. "Actually, I have several."

"Such as?" he asked cautiously.

Addy absently tucked a wayward strand of hair that had escaped from her chignon behind her ear and said, "First of all, the small size of the pool."

"The pool?" Joe tore his gaze away from the way the dark red curl was snuggled against her slim neck. What she was saying was difficult enough to follow without his getting sidetracked.

"Of eligible men to marry," she explained patiently. "Most of the good ones are already taken. And I don't have the—" she gestured ineffectually "—the ability to attract the few who are available."

Joe allowed his eyes to roam down the length of her body. "I wouldn't be too sure of that," he murmured.

Addy swallowed, trying to ignore the way her skin prickled under his stare. "I'm not talking about grabbing their attention. I'm talking about maintaining it long enough for a relationship to develop. The plain truth is that eligible men make me tongue-tied. I know I'm not overweight anymore on the outside, but inside I still feel awkward and unattractive."

Joe studied her, surprised by her admission, although he could certainly relate to it. He had more money than anyone in this damn town and yet he still felt socially inferior at any gathering.

"I have no experience with making small talk with men," she plowed on when he didn't say anything. "With the kind of sexual banter that every other woman I know seems to have learned in grade school. I don't know what men like or how they think or what they expect from a date...."

"It can't be that bad." Joe felt an urge to comfort her. To put his arms around her and wipe away the uncertainty darkening her eyes.

Addy grimaced. "Do you know how many dates I've

had in my life? I'll tell you," she rushed on before he could say anything. "Three. Exactly three. One in high school and the twit parked the car on the side of the road and demanded sex."

"His technique left a lot to be desired, even for a high-school kid," Joe said dryly.

"Technique nothing. He told me that anyone as fat as I was should be grateful to trade sex for a date."

"The little bastard!" Joe felt a flash of anger at Addy's bleak expression.

"Definitely. Anyway, I slapped him and walked home. My second date was during nurse's training and all he wanted to talk about was his microbes. I doubt that I even registered as a woman to him. I was simply an audience who was too unsure of herself to tell him that I found him boring as the devil."

Joe chuckled. "You said three. What about the third?"

"The son of a patient I nursed. His mother was an unstable diabetic, and he was divorced with two teenagers, one of whom was pregnant and the other one was strung out on drugs. He saw me as the answer to all his problems. A nurse to take care of his family."

Joe shook his head. "The man was blind."

"Desperate," Addy corrected, "but what I was trying to make you understand was that I have no experience at dating. And if I'm going to have any luck at finding a husband, I'm going to have to get some."

"What ever happened to looking across a room and falling madly in love?"

"I did that once," Addy assured him seriously. "At a hospital dance. As usual, I was standing on the sidelines trying to pretend that I was waiting for someone who just hadn't shown up yet. Then I looked over at the refreshment table and saw the most gorgeous man. Every hormone I had went into overdrive."

"What happened?"

"I mentioned him to a girlfriend of mine later in the

evening, and she said that he was a disbarred lawyer who was at the hospital doing community service that had been ordered by the court because he'd been convicted of embezzling funds from his elderly clients. That took the shine off my feelings.''

"I rather imagine it might. All right, I'll concede that you have no experience at dating, but what does that have to do with your property?'' Joe decided to risk finding out if he was the husband she had in mind.

Addy ran her tongue over her lower lip, took a deep breath and blurted out her plan. "I'll sell you my property if you'll let me practice dating skills on you.''

Joe blinked, taken aback. "Exactly what do I have to do?'' he asked cautiously.

"Well... I thought... If we were to have some dates, then I could practice relating to a man. And you could tell me how men feel about various things. That way when I went out with a real candidate, I'd have some first-hand knowledge of how the male mind works.''

Joe stared down at his drink as he considered her crazy idea. But the more he thought about it, the saner it seemed. Addy had identified her goal, as well as what it was that was keeping her from reaching that goal, and she'd thought out a logical way to remedy her lack. Her reasoning was impeccable. What she really wanted was a combination brother and Dutch uncle. He glanced up into her soft, brown eyes, which were watching him hopefully.

He could help her, he told himself. It wasn't as if she were trying to marry *him*. Which made sense because he'd always known that his main attraction for women was his money, and Addy didn't care about money.

No, Addy wasn't a threat to his blissfully single state. And she was his friend, he reminded himself. And while he didn't have a great deal of experience with friends, even he knew that friends helped each other out. His eyes homed in on the soft, pink fullness of her lips. Would his tutelage include kissing her? The idea shook his composure.

Her land. He dragged his mind back to the central issue with an effort.

"It's an intriguing idea," he said slowly, "but there's a problem from my perspective. I need your property now, not at some time in the future when you finally manage to lure some hapless male to the altar."

Addy tried to ignore her sense of discouragement at his immediate judgment that it would take her a long time to find a husband, focusing instead on the rest of his words. "But if I sell you my home, then I won't have any place to live," she pointed out. "And—"

"Damn!" Joe's roughly bitten-off expletive interrupted her. He was staring at a point over her left shoulder, an annoyed expression on his face.

Addy started to turn around to see what had caught his attention.

"Don't look," he ordered. "It's Charlie Wheeling. Come on." He stood up and held out a hand for her. "Let's dance. Maybe he'll take the hint and go away."

Addy put her hand in his and stood up, suddenly full of inhibitions. "I can't dance," she hissed as he led her out onto the crowded, postage-stamp-sized dance floor. "I never learned."

"You aren't about to learn here, either. There isn't room. Just follow me."

Addy did as she was told, instinctively moving closer as he took her in his arms. The heat from his body reached out to engulf her, warming her flesh and softening her muscles. She felt pliable. As if she could mold herself to him. Another couple bumped into them and Joe gathered her even closer, cradling her protectively against him. Her breasts brushed against his chest, sending a tingling sensation shooting through her. She could feel the tips stiffening, and she had to fight an impulse to move closer to try to intensify the sensation.

Addy took a deep, steadying breath, but it only made matters worse. The scent of his cologne filled her nostrils.

He smelled so good, she thought dreamily. Not overpowering, the way some men did, but subtle. As if he were hiding most of his personality from the casual observer. As he probably was, she realized with a flash of insight. Joe Barrington was a very private person. What would it be like to probe behind the face he presented to the world? The tantalizing idea caught her off guard and she stumbled, falling against Joe's chest. It was like hitting a warm wall. There was no give to him anywhere. He must be pure muscle. What would he look like without his clothes on? The images that flooded her mind flustered her and she stumbled again.

Still, she decided she'd much rather Joe thought she was clumsy than so susceptible to his nearness. It was only propinquity, after all, she tried to tell herself. She'd been thinking about men and sex and marriage and children for over two weeks now, and Joe was an attractive man. A very attractive man. It was hardly surprising that she would react to being this near to him.

"Oh, hell!" Joe bit out. "Wheeling sat down at our table. Can you believe that? The jerk is going to wait for us."

Addy glanced back at their table. The man seated in Joe's chair looked pretty harmless to her. "Maybe he just wants to say hello?"

Joe gave her a cynical look that chilled her. "Charlie sells insurance, and he's been after me to buy my liability insurance from him for months."

"Tell him no and be done with it. As long as you keep avoiding him, he'll hope you'll eventually agree."

"I did say no, the first time he asked, so now he's switched his tactics. He keeps inviting me to things."

Addy studied Joe's annoyed features thoughtfully. Apparently she wasn't the only one who couldn't throw off the past. Joe appeared to assume that a social invitation automatically came with strings attached. That no one could want him just because they enjoyed his company.

"Have you ever considered that he might simply want to get to know you better?" Addy suggested.

"No."

"Well, consider it now."

Joe narrowed his eyes, stared briefly at the ceiling and then said, "Okay. I considered it, and I still don't believe it."

"You're far too cynical."

"And you're far too trusting," he countered. "I suppose it comes of your being so hung up on religion. You've started to believe what they tell you."

"I am not hung up on religion!" she objected. "I simply happen to believe in the value system that my particular religion espouses. And one of those values is that one should give the benefit of the doubt to people."

"Hung up," he repeated. "If you'd take a good look around you, you'd see that people aren't very nice."

"They are too! Most of them," she amended.

"You need a reality check. Come on." Taking her arm, Joe shepherded her back to their table.

"I'm going to introduce you to Charlie. That should be enough to convince even you."

"Joe!" Charlie got to his feet as they approached and, giving them a wide grin, held out his hand. "My wife saw you when we came in and she told me that I should come over and invite you to a party we're having this weekend. Kind of a coming-out party for her cousin Warren."

"Where's he been?" Addy asked cautiously, fearing the worst. She was fast coming to the conclusion that Joe had been right. Her gut reaction to Wheeling was distaste. He was simply too...something.

"Married. His divorce becomes final next week. So we thought we'd throw a party and celebrate his freedom. You're invited too, Miss..."

"Edson," Joe introduced her. "Addy, this is Charlie Wheeling."

Charlie frowned at her. "I vaguely remember an Edson

from high school, but you couldn't be her. She was fat and..."

Addy stared at him as anger and embarrassment surged through her. She wanted to yell at him and run and hide at the same time.

"Oh, sorry. No offense intended..." Charlie stammered. "I didn't mean..."

"I'll get back to you about the party," Joe said, cutting him off.

"Sure. Anytime." Charlie hurriedly escaped.

"Yes?" Joe gave her a wicked grin. "You were telling me what a good guy he was."

Addy sank down into her chair. "People who go around saying 'I told you so,' are universally disliked."

"But at least they don't get taken advantage of. Or insulted."

"Maybe he didn't mean to be insulting." Addy tried to be fair, even though Charlie's comment burned in her mind. "After all, I was fat in school. All he did was state a fact."

"There are lots of facts that are better left unsaid, and one would expect someone his age to have figured that out."

"It would have been nice. Who's he married to?"

"The bleached blonde sitting beside him."

Addy turned and looked to find a vaguely familiar woman staring at her. The woman smiled and waved, and Addy politely waved back as she tried to place her.

"When you knew her, she was Cookie Lawton," Joe offered.

Addy's mouth dropped open in shock. "That's Cookie Lawton! She's at least seventy-five pounds heavier than she was in school and she looks...artificial."

Joe shook his head and gave her a mournful look which was belied by the twinkle in his eyes. "Shame on you. Taking pleasure in the fact that one of the social lions of your high-school class has gone to seed."

"I wasn't..." Addy began and then giggled enchantingly. "Yes, I was. If you only knew how many years I put up with her sly little digs about whales during gym classes, and now to find out that she's overweight..."

"While you look like the embodiment of every man's dream," Joe finished.

Addy stared at him uncertainly, wondering if he was just saying what he thought she wanted to hear, or if he might actually like how she looked.

"As long as the dream doesn't turn into a nightmare," she finally said. "Now, about what we were talking about before Charlie interrupted?"

"Yes, nightmares and marriage do kind of go together."

"Don't be facetious," she said. "I'm serious. Will you help me?" She held her breath, mentally willing him to do it.

Joe stared down into the melting ice cubes in his drink for a long moment and then said, "As I was saying, I need your land now."

"Yeah, I remember." Addy felt her spirits sink.

"There is a way around it, though," he said slowly. "I live in the old Iverson place."

"I think I remember it. Isn't it that huge old Queen Anne place sitting on most of a city block over on North Washington?"

"That's it. It was in pretty bad shape when I bought it, and I had it virtually rebuilt inside. There was also a housekeeper's cottage in the back by the garage that was redone at the same time. But, since I prefer my privacy, I use a cleaning service and the cottage has never been occupied. You could stay there."

Addy was taken aback by his offer. Apparently he didn't think that she was enough of a threat to his privacy to matter. For some reason the thought rankled. Just once, she'd like a man to consider her a massive threat to his peace of mind. Someday, she promised herself. And accepting Joe's offer was the first step on the road to that someday. She took a deep breath, trying to keep her focus on the future and not the past and said, "It's a deal."

"I'll have my lawyers draw up the papers first thing in the morning, and you can stop by the plant about ten and sign them."

Addy chuckled. "You mean, here's your hat, what's your hurry?"

"The sooner you sign, the sooner I can get started on the new plant," he defended himself. "Also the sooner we can get started on your project." His eyes narrowed, and he stared past her.

Addy, who was coming to recognize what she thought of as his thinking mode, waited.

"Maybe we ought to go," he finally said.

"Go?" Addy frowned. "Go where?"

"To the Wheelings' party. It'll give you a chance to look over the competition."

"How so?" Addy asked, not understanding.

"If the party is to reintroduce Warren to the social scene, then it makes sense that all the eligible women that the Wheelings know will be there."

"Clever." Addy gave credit where it was due. "But I would have thought that you already know the competition?" She couldn't resist the gentle probe into his private life.

"I haven't the time for parties. Nor the stomach," he said bitterly. "You know damn well Cookie Wheeling would never have invited me if it weren't for my money. She practically held her skirts away from me in school when I passed her in the halls so that I wouldn't contaminate her."

Addy felt her heart twist at his revealing words. Somehow, she'd never thought of Joe as caring what the others thought of him. But obviously she'd been wrong.

"Joe..." she began, not sure what she should say. What she could say. Only knowing that she wanted to ease his pain.

A wry smile curved his lips. "Please, spare me the consoling homily."

"I wasn't going to give you one. I was merely going to point out that people change. Everything changes."

"Yeah, particularly my financial worth."

"Quit harping about your money!"

"Why not, when it's my major appeal to people?"

"And don't talk in generalities! I could give a hang about your money."

"Which makes you the exception that proves the rule."

Addy shook her head in annoyance and gave up. He wasn't going to listen to her. Maybe she could find some way of showing him. It would be a fitting reward for helping her.

"About the Wheelings' party," Joe persisted.

Addy bit back her instinctive refusal and tried to think. If she was going to find a husband, then sooner or later she was going to have to face the social scene. It might as well be sooner. And Joe would be there. Her spirits rose fractionally. She wouldn't have to face the situation on her own.

"I think you're right," she finally said.

"I usually am," he said with a smugness that made her smile. Joe was such a strange mixture. She had never really realized what a complex man he was. Getting to know him again was going to be an intriguing process.

Three

"Change is the essence of life," Addy muttered to herself as she closed the back door of her parents' home behind her and headed toward her car. Climbing behind the wheel, she turned on the ignition and pulled away.

Unable to resist the temptation, she stopped at the end of the driveway and stared back at the house. For a moment, an overwhelming feeling of grief filled her at all that she'd lost. Of the people who had lived there that she'd never see again. Then the feeling of intense sadness ebbed, leaving room for memories to surface. Memories of sitting beside her grandmother at the kitchen table and sneaking sips of her coffee when her mother wasn't looking. Memories of her mother standing at the stove cooking supper while Addy perched on a stool and told her all about her school day. Memories of sitting on the old rocker on the front porch and waiting for her father to come home from work.

Addy closed her eyes, relishing the feeling of warmth

and love that always came when she thought of her parents. It was a feeling she could call up anytime, she suddenly realized. The feeling was part of her. She didn't need the house to bring it to mind.

Addy nodded decisively, feeling fractionally better about her decision to sell. It really was time to move on. She pulled out into the road. Would her children someday remember her with the same sense of happiness with which she remembered her parents? She pondered the unsettling idea as she covered the short distance to Joe's plant.

The visitors' parking spaces in front of the plant were filled, so Addy drove around to the back of the building and parked there. Making sure that her car door was locked, she started toward the offices, only to pause when she noticed a sign that said Nurse's Office. Wondering what kind of facilities Joe provided for his workers, Addy pushed the door open and stepped inside.

She found herself in a starkly sterile room. The walls were painted an antiseptic white and an institutional light gray tile covered the floor. Except for six gray plastic chairs lined up against the wall, the room was empty. There were no magazines, no plants. Nothing to relieve the oppressive barrenness.

Addy shivered. It might be adequate for treating the body, but the room was a total flop at providing comfort to the senses.

Curious as to what type of person was content to work in these bleak surroundings, Addy walked toward the open door at the back of the room labeled Nurse. She was about to knock when she heard a sharp, feminine voice from inside snap, "No! It isn't my job."

The woman was answered by a softly apologetic male voice, "But I just want to know what to do about all the ear infections my son has."

"My job is to treat accidents that occur in the workplace, not to be giving you advice on raising your kids."

Addy frowned. What kind of nurse had Joe hired? Any

professional worth her salt should be happy to pass on any health information that might help.

"Go see a doctor," the woman continued, "and quit wasting my time."

"I have." The man's voice sharpened. "But he just prescribes something and, when I try to get information, he brushes me off."

Rather like the nurse here, Addy thought.

"That's not my problem," the woman said. "It's time for my break."

Addy hurriedly left, not wanting to be caught eavesdropping. It would appear that there were some gaps in the health service that Joe's company provided. And dangerous ones, too. Sometimes, information could be more important than a prescription—a fact that father had instinctively known. Not that his insight appeared to be doing him much good.

Addy frowned thoughtfully as she pushed open the doors to the factory's main offices. She was at loose ends at the moment. She had intended to see if she couldn't do some volunteer work for one of the various social agencies in town, but maybe she wouldn't have to go that far. It appeared to her that there was real need right here for someone with her skills. The plant needed a children's clinic. She could include regular checkups and classes dealing with various children's health issues.

If Joe would let her do it. Reality put the brakes on her enthusiasm. He might not be willing to let her use the facilities of his clinic. He might not want to upset his nurse by bringing in someone else.

Addy chewed thoughtfully on her lower lip. She didn't know what he would say, but she did know that the very worst thing that would happen would be that he would say no. In which case, she wouldn't be any worse off than she was. And he might well say yes. Joe was such a strange mixture of hardheaded cynicism and caring, it was impossible to tell what his reaction to her request might be.

"Ah, Miss Edson." The immaculately groomed receptionist gave her a bright, professional smile. "Mr. Barrington said that you would be stopping by this morning. He said to send you right through to his office."

"Thank you." Addy resisted the impulse to check the front of her lemon-yellow shirt for dirt smudges. She wondered how long it took the woman each morning to achieve such polished perfection. It was probably an inherited trait, she thought glumly, like being born with musical ability.

Addy started down the hall, her footsteps unconsciously quickening at the thought of seeing Joe. She entered the reception area outside his office, pausing when she realized that she wasn't the only person waiting.

There was a thin, harassed-looking man who appeared to be in his late thirties sitting in a brown leather chair. His head was bent, and he was staring fixedly at the design in the Oriental carpet. His shoulders were hunched defensively as if he were expecting a blow, and Addy's soft heart was touched. Poor soul, she thought, and went over to sit down across from him, intending to distract him from his obviously unhappy thoughts.

"Good morning," she said cheerfully.

The man jumped and gave her an uncertain smile.

"It hasn't been, so far," he muttered. He glanced worriedly at the door to Joe's office and then down at his watch. "What time is your appointment with Barrington for?"

"Well, I don't actually have one," Addy said. "I'm just here to sign a few papers. Is he running late?"

"That's one way of putting it. My appointment was for almost an hour ago." He sighed despondently. "Which probably means that he isn't all that interested in our meeting."

"Not necessarily. Maybe he got an overseas call. Or maybe he spilled coffee all over his suit and he had to send it out to get cleaned and he's waiting for it to come back."

Which would mean that he was sitting there in his underwear, Addy thought, as her mind followed her nonsense through to its logical conclusion. What kind of underwear did Joe wear? The tantalizing thought drifted through her mind. Silk boxer shorts? Soft and smooth and eminently touchable? Or perhaps plain white cotton briefs that would fit snugly over his—

The man's chuckle broke into her erotic thoughts, and she blinked, refocusing on the man.

"Thank you, Miss—" He paused expectantly.

"Edson. Addy Edson," she responded, rather surprised at how easily she'd handled the move from stranger to introduced stranger. Of course, there was nothing even remotely sexual in their encounter, she conceded. But even so, any conversation with a man was good practice.

"I'm David Edwards." He held out a hand, and Addy shook it.

"I—" he began and then broke off as the door opened and Joe appeared.

Addy turned, David Edwards forgotten at the sight of Joe.

He was wearing another of those impeccably tailored suits. Its pale gray material hugged his shoulders, subtly emphasizing their width. The pristine whiteness of his cotton shirt emphasized his light tan, and Addy felt her fingers itch with a desire to rub her fingers over his cheek to see if it was as smooth as it looked. She automatically clenched her fingers to try to dispel the urge, unsettled by the intensity of her physical reaction.

"Mr. Barrington," David began, only to be cut off by Joe's curt nod.

"Edwards," Joe said. "I'll be with you in a minute."

"I don't mind waiting, and you were here first." Addy gave David an encouraging smile. If Joe didn't put the man out of his misery pretty soon, she was liable to get to practice her CPR skills on him.

To her surprise, Joe scowled at her. "I'll see Edwards after you."

"That's okay," David assured her, and Addy, confused by the undercurrents she could feel but didn't understand, followed Joe into his office.

Addy watched him curiously as he closed his door with a decided snap. "I really don't have anything else to do."

"He can wait."

"But should he?" She probed Joe's tense attitude.

"Have you got a hankering for the country-club set?"

"I am not a snob, but I'm beginning to have my doubts about you," Addy replied, defending herself.

"Me!" Joe looked dumbfounded.

"You sound very much like a reverse snob," she insisted. "Either variety is a pain."

Joe pressed his lips together and glared at her. "You don't understand."

"That much is clear," she conceded. "So explain."

Joe shoved his long fingers through his thick, dark hair and finally said, "Do you know who he is?"

"He said his name was David Edwards. Isn't it?"

"Yes." Joe bit the word off.

"Is there supposed to be some special significance to his name?" she finally asked, thoroughly confused.

"You don't remember the son of the town's leading citizen?" he mocked. "He owns that huge, white, pillared place just south of town."

"Oh, that Edwards." Addy shrugged. "I don't think I ever meet him before. Is he a competitor of yours?" she asked, trying to figure out why Joe disliked the man so.

"Hardly!" Joe's tone was scathing. "He's got no more business sense than you do."

Addy looked down her nose at him. "There is no need to be so superior. For all I know I could have lots of business sense. I simply have no interest in finding out. And, besides, having business sense is not a measure of character."

"I told you," Joe said tightly, "he's an Edwards."

"So you did. What you didn't tell me was why being born an Edwards should qualify him as a social pariah."

Joe stared at her, his eyes narrowed to blue slits. Addy stared back, refusing to be intimidated by his forbidding demeanor. This was Joe, she reminded herself. Her old friend.

"Don't get mixed up with the bastard," Joe ordered.

"Chance would be a fine thing," she said dryly.

"I saw the way he was looking at you," Joe insisted. "Like he's just found a friendly face."

"Well, he had," Addy pointed out reasonably. "Why don't you like the guy? Does he cheat on his income tax?"

"Can't you just take my word for it?" Joe said in exasperation.

"No," she said succinctly, feeling a strange exhilaration in arguing with Joe. "Part of relating to a man is learning how to have meaningful discussions. This is a meaningful discussion."

Joe stared at her for a long moment as if considering his options, and just when Addy was beginning to think that he wasn't going to say anything else, he dropped a bombshell.

"David Edwards is my half brother."

Addy opened her mouth, closed it, swallowed and then muttered, "Run that by me again."

"We have the same father but different mothers," Joe elaborated.

Addy dropped into the chair across from Joe's desk and simply stared at him, having a great deal of trouble taking it all in. "I never heard anything about it before," she finally said.

"As far as I know, no one else knew. My mother went to work for Edwards right out of secretarial school, and he promptly seduced her into an affair. When she got pregnant a couple of years later, he broke the relationship off and abandoned her."

Addy winced at the pain she could see reflected deep in

his eyes. She desperately wanted to say something to erase that pain, but she couldn't think of a single thing that might work.

"I'd like smack the pair of them up alongside the head," she said, "but since they're both dead..."

Joe glanced toward his closed door. "What are you talking about? Andrew Edwards is dead, but David isn't."

"I was referring to your parents."

"It wasn't my mother's fault! I told you. Edwards seduced her."

Addy studied his outraged features for a long moment, debating whether to change the subject or persist in a line of reasoning that was sure to make him mad. No, madder. He was already mad. Persist, she finally decided. This whole mess was eating away at Joe. That much was obvious, and until he came to terms with what had happened all those years ago, he was never going to be free of it. Maybe she could help him overcome it. It was the least she could do considering what he was doing for her.

"Unless Edwards raped her, then your mother has to bear part of the responsibility," Addy said carefully.

Apparently not carefully enough. Joe scowled at her. "He was fifteen years older than she was."

"Granted, but she was an adult. There is no way she couldn't have known that the man had a wife at home, and yet she still had an affair with him."

"She loved him," Joe insisted, "and he repaid her love by destroying her life. By turning her into a drunk."

Addy slowly shook her head. "No one made your mother drink, Joe. She chose to handle her problems by drinking. Just as she chose to start an affair and to continue it for years even though it should have been obvious that Edwards had no intention of leaving his wife. I don't remember your mother, but—"

"She was a pathetic victim of Edwards. She never even left the house. She simply hid in her room and drank to hide her sorrow and shame."

Addy frowned. "Then how did she pay her bills?"

"What?"

"I just wondered how she paid her bills? Did Edwards support the pair of you?"

"Support! He never gave her a damn thing."

"He gave her you."

"You don't understand." His plaint struck Addy as curiously childlike. But then Joe's whole response to his parents was rooted in childhood. Maybe even locked in childhood. Judging from his reaction to David Edwards, it was going to take some time before he ever got to the point where he could be rational about it. And she had probably pushed enough for one day.

"I guess I don't," she finally said. "At any rate, I came by to see if you had the papers ready for me to sign."

Joe stared at her, frustrated by her refusal to see his mother as the victim she was. Finally, he decided to drop it for the time being. Surely after Addy had had time to think it over, she'd realize he was right.

He rummaged through the papers on his desk and pulled out a file. "I used the last offering price as the selling price, okay?"

"Fine, where do I sign?"

"You should have your lawyer look it over first."

Addy grinned at him. "Why? Were you planning on cheating me?"

Joe frowned disapprovingly at her. "You shouldn't trust anyone, including me."

"What a depressing philosophy. Give me the papers, and I'll sign."

"I guess it's all right," he said slowly. "I know I'm not cheating you."

"That makes two of us," she said cheerfully, signing where he pointed.

"Here's a key to the cottage." He handed her a set of keys. "Everything is in working order. At least, it was when I signed off on it two years ago," he added.

"Now he tells me," she said wryly, shoving the keys into her jeans pocket.

"I'll run you over and show you the place." Joe got to his feet.

Addy's desire to spend time with Joe fought with her sense of fairness at leaving David Edwards stranded. Her sense of fairness won. "You still have to see David."

"Let him wait."

"Not on my account. But if you want to do something for me..." Addy paused, wondering if this was a good time to broach her desire to work in his clinic. Her failure to sympathize with his mother's circumstances might make him resistant. Mentally, she shrugged. He could only refuse.

Joe eyed her cautiously, wondering what more she wanted from him. Addy was so very different from the women he'd had much to do with in the past. They'd only wanted things. Things that took no more effort to grant than writing a check. Addy's favors seemed to involve a great deal of personal effort on his part. But even so, he couldn't quite bring himself to squelch her, to douse the enthusiasm he could see shinning in her eyes.

"What exactly is it you want?" he asked.

"For you to say yes." Addy grinned at him, and Joe felt a curious sense of lightness ease the tension he'd been feeling from his hectic morning.

"What do you know about your factory's medical facilities?" she asked.

Joe blinked, trying to figure out in advance where the conversation was headed. He couldn't. "We have a nurse to handle minor problems. For anything serious, we call an ambulance."

"Well, I want you to let me include child care for your employees' families."

"You want me to hire you?" Joe studied her speculatively as he weighed the idea of her working for him. Of her being around every day. Of her taking his orders, doing as he wished. No, reality scotched the idea. Addy wasn't likely to take his orders unless it suited her, no matter what he was paying her.

"No," she said. "I consider learning how to go about finding a husband to be my full-time job for the present. What I want to do is volunteer work in your clinic to keep my nursing skills sharp.

"And since your own nurse's area of expertise is in industrial nursing, I doubt that she would have either the interest or the background to run a baby clinic."

Joe considered her words. "You don't like the nurse in my clinic," he finally decided.

"It isn't for me to like or dislike her." Addy refused to criticize a colleague. "All I want to do is to run a baby clinic and answer parents' questions about their children. It's a job that I really enjoy, and there appears to be a need for it. All I need from you is permission to use your facilities."

Joe shrugged. "I doubt very much that I'll get off that easily, since both the government and the unions are involved. Tell you what, I'll ask the company's lawyer about it. If he doesn't see any legal problems, you can."

"You'll call him today? As soon as you've seen David Edwards?"

Joe gave her a wolfish smile. "I'll call before I see Edwards."

"After will be soon enough." She got to her feet and headed toward the door.

"I'll let you know what the verdict is when I pick you up this evening."

Addy felt a spurt of excitement. She paused and looked back at him, her eyes lingering on the gleam in his eyes. "Are you picking me up this evening?" she asked, trying to sound businesslike about it.

"If we're going to go to the Wheelings' party this weekend, you'd better get in all the practice you can before then.

Besides, there's nothing to be gained by waiting. You aren't getting any younger.''

Addy frowned at him. "And you aren't getting any more tactful. I've still got a few good years left.'' She jerked open the door and marched out. Not getting any younger indeed, she fumed.

Joe watched her leave with a smile twitching the corners of his mouth. Who would have thought that Addy would be sensitive about her age? But she was wrong about one thing. She didn't have a few good years left. She had lots of good years left. Addy was the kind of woman who would still be as interesting when she was ninety as she was today. And probably as sexy.

And she was sexy. He swallowed as he remembered the alluring sway of her body as she'd stalked out. His eyes narrowed the better to hold the enticing image sharp in his mind as he tried to figure out just why he found her so seductive.

Her appeal wasn't the blatant attraction of a woman showing off her body to anyone who cared to look. She didn't seem to employ any of the artifices his girlfriends had used on him over the years. She didn't deliberately touch him or give him tantalizing glimpses of her anatomy to whet his appetite. Hell, he doubted that Addy even knew how to manipulate either her own femininity or his basic sexual responses.

So why did he find himself indulging in erotic fantasies every time he saw her? He wasn't sure. He just knew that he wanted to delve deeper into the question. Much deeper. What would it be like to make love to her? he wondered. To pull her naked body beneath his? To feel her soft breasts pressing into his bare chest? He shifted restlessly as his body began to harden at his provocative thoughts.

Bill stuck his head in through the open door. "Are you ready to see Mr. Edwards now, Joe?''

Joe frowned as he suddenly remembered that Edwards was waiting.

"I need you to call our lawyer and find out if there's any government regulations or union agreements that would prohibit a volunteer from holding baby clinics on the premises for our employees. If there isn't, tell him to make sure our insurance covers it."

Bill, never slow on the uptake, immediately made the connection. "Miss Edson?"

Joe's mouth lifted in a curiously tender smile. "Right in one. Apparently, Addy is going to have a go at changing our little corner of the world.

"And send in Edwards." Joe's voice hardened, and Bill gratefully withdrew.

Addy spent the afternoon moving into the cottage. By seven o'clock, she'd finished her shower and was standing in front of her closet trying to decide what she should be wearing for their first practice date.

Her all-too-familiar sense of social inadequacy began to dampen her mood of anticipation. According to what Kathy had said, Joe's last girlfriend had been a high-fashion model.

Addy stared at her meager wardrobe, hanging in lonely splendor in the oversized closet. Not one piece of it even approached high fashion. And not only that, but he'd already seen the best she had to offer at dinner last night. She pushed her green silk to one side. She couldn't wear the same dress twice in a row. Which meant her choices were limited to two. One was a very pretty yellow silk print that she'd bought before she'd gone to Africa. Before she'd lost the last fifty pounds. Which meant that the dress gaped around her neck, bunched at her waist and hung very strangely.

First chance she got, she'd have to drive down to Philadelphia and see about replenishing her wardrobe. Definitely before the Wheelings' party. After all, she couldn't go fishing without some kind of bait, she told herself, and then giggled at the idea of covering herself with feathers like a fishing lure.

Or better yet, covering her quarry with feathers. She blinked as an image of Joe wearing feathers and nothing else popped into her mind. Maybe a cloak of feathers. Bloodred and bright yellow ones like in the cloaks those long-ago warrior kings of Hawaii had worn. And maybe a few blue ones for contrast. Worn a little lower. Her breathing shortened as she imagined exactly where she would place them.

Oh, yes, she thought dreamily. Joe would make wonderful bait. But not for someone as inexperienced as she was. She brought her wayward imagination up short. Joe was the means to an end, not the end itself, she reminded herself.

With a feeling of regret that vaguely worried her, Addy pulled out a subdued-looking gray dress that she'd bought to wear to official events at the convent. About the only positive thing she could say about it was that it fit. Sighing, she slipped into it.

She was carefully applying lipstick when the sharp sound of the doorbell suddenly bludgeoned her eardrums. Her hand jerked, and she smeared the lipstick. "Drat!" she muttered in annoyance. Joe was here, and she wasn't ready yet. She glanced down at her watch as she hurriedly jammed her feet into her shoes. Although, maybe it wasn't Joe. He'd said that he'd pick her up at seven and it was only six-forty. Maybe it was someone else.

Addy opened the door to find Joe standing on the doorstep and a feeling of pleasure washed over her. Unfortunately, her pleasure didn't last past his greeting.

"That dress makes you look jaundiced."

Addy gestured into the small living room. "Come in and get comfortable while you insult me."

"I'm not insulting you," he insisted. "I'm instructing you on what men like."

"All men can't like the same thing. Some men probably like this color."

"A necrophiliac comes to mind!" he shot back. "And what's that on your face?" He leaned over her, and Addy felt overwhelmed by his physical presence. She could feel the heat from his body encircling her and the faintly spicy tang of his cologne trickling into her lungs.

"Face?" she muttered, her mind too full of how he made her feel to pay much attention to what he was saying.

"There." He reached out and touched the sensitive skin near the corner of her mouth with his forefinger.

Addy jumped as a shower of sparks skidded through her, sensitizing her skin even further.

"Sit still," he ordered. "I don't bite."

Too bad, Addy thought irreverently. Playing out a vampire fantasy with Joe would be quite an experience.

She resisted the compulsion to lean toward him and waited as he pulled a spotless white handkerchief out of his pocket and dabbed at the smear on her face.

"There," he muttered.

"Thanks." Addy's voice came out sounding high and breathless, and she hurriedly stepped back to put some space between them.

She looked at him uncertainly, wondering what the proper protocol was once you got your date inside.

"Why are you staring at me as if I'd suddenly grown a second head?" he asked.

"Don't you dare turn paranoid on me. I'm uncertain enough for both of us. I was just trying to figure out what I was supposed to do now that my date was in my living room."

Joe grinned at her. "In the interest of accuracy, you're in *my* living room."

Addy frowned at him. "That brings up possibilities that I don't even want to consider. Tell me, how am I supposed to find out what you have in mind for the evening without sounding..." She gestured impotently.

"You could try asking."

"All right." Addy took a deep breath, fixed her gaze on the devilment she could see gleaming deep in his eyes and said, "What did you have in mind for us to do this evening?"

Joe felt a sudden shock of desire slam through him at the thought of what he'd really like to do with her this evening. He'd like to take her in his arms and kiss her senseless. To learn the exact shape and taste of her mouth. He'd like to strip that god-awful dress off her and run his hands over her body. He'd like to explore the silky texture of her skin. He clenched his fingers into fists as his body began to react to his desires.

But even if he couldn't go that far, there was no reason why he shouldn't kiss her. Kissing was a normal part of dating and this was supposed to be a date. All he needed to do was to be casual about it. Addy didn't have a clue about normal dating procedures, so she wouldn't object. Maybe it would give him an insight into why he found her so sexy and once he'd figured that out, maybe it would lessen his physical reaction to her. At least he hoped so, he thought ruefully. He hadn't spent so much time aroused since he'd been a teenager. And he was finding it a damned uncomfortable state to be in. At least it was when he knew that he couldn't follow his desires through to their logical end.

"I hadn't really thought that far ahead," he said, taking refuge in a lie. "What would you like to do?"

"That's not fair! How can I figure out how much money the guy has to spend if he doesn't suggest something first?"

"I have more money than you could spend in two lifetimes," Joe said flatly.

"Yeah, but you aren't typical. Most men have limited means."

"If they haven't the gumption to speak up and tell you what they want to do, then they deserve to get stuck with the bill for what you want."

"Wait a minute. You make it sound like anything that I want to do wouldn't be something that a man would want to do. Men are every bit as different as women. What do you like?"

"I don't like Broadway plays, operas, the ballet and the latest 'in' restaurant that serves tiny portions of something with an incomprehensible name that smells like mildew. That's what my dates all want to do."

"If you know that and you continue to ask them out, then you deserve to be stuck with evenings you don't like," Addy replied. "But I must say you aren't being much help. Don't tell me what you *don't* want to do. Tell me what you *do* want to do."

"I want to eat and relax in that order. It's been a helluva day. Which reminds me, my lawyer gave the okay on your clinic. You can start anytime you want."

"Thanks!" Addy beamed at him. "And I have no objection to staying home this evening, but I can't cook anything for you. I didn't get to the store."

Joe looked around the sparsely furnished living room. It boasted neither a television nor a VCR. "Let's go up to my place," he said. "We can order a pizza and watch a movie." Which should give him ample opportunity to get her into his arms.

"You're on," Addy agreed, eager to see what kind of home he'd created for himself.

Four

___

Joe opened his front door, gesturing Addy inside.

"Make yourself at home while I check my messages," he said as he disappeared down the hall.

Intensely curious, Addy walked across the black-and-white marble tile of the intimidatingly elegant foyer and peered into the large room to her right. It was a living room evidently designed for use by beautiful people who didn't have anything as messy as kids or pets.

The room had been decorated in shades of white, ranging from the matching eight-foot cream sofas in front of the white marble fireplace, to the off-white Berber carpet that covered the floor. The only color came from the wood tables and a few accent pieces.

Addy barely suppressed a shudder at the room's sterility. It might be beautiful in the abstract, but it definitely wasn't welcoming. She turned as Joe came back.

"What do you want on your pizza?" Joe asked, picking

up the ivory-and-gold phone sitting beside an overstuffed cream-colored chair.

Addy opened her mouth to say that any kind of veggie would be fine, when she suddenly realized that a man would probably want meat. Should she tell Joe what she really wanted or should she pretend that she wanted to eat what he ordered?

"It doesn't matter," she said, deciding to take the line of least resistance.

Joe set the phone down with a snap. "First lesson," he said. "I hate that. Most men hate that."

"Hate what?"

"The cop-out of putting the decision of what to order on me."

"I thought men liked to be assertive?"

Joe shrugged. "About some things we do. In bed, for example."

In bed? His words echoed curiously in Addy's ears, and her eyes dropped to his mouth, lingering on the pulsating warmth of his lips. How assertive was assertive? And what did assertive in bed cover? His partner? Her heartbeat suddenly went into overdrive.

"When a man asks for your input, assume that he wants it and give it to him."

Addy blinked, trying to focus on his words. "All right. I prefer veggies. The reason I didn't say anything was that I assumed that you'd be heavily into sausage or some such."

"Pepperoni, but that's easily fixed. We'll get half pepperoni and half veggies. Okay?"

Addy smiled at him. "Okay."

She wandered over to the French doors on the far wall while he called their order in. He knew the number of the pizza place by heart, she realized, wondering what kind of diet he normally ate. It wasn't her business, she told herself, looking out onto the brick patio with its huge pots of bushy red dahlias.

"What are you staring at?" Joe asked. Walking over, he peered over her shoulder.

Addy ran the tip of her tongue over her suddenly dry lips as a skittery feeling chased over her skin. Even though Joe wasn't actually touching her, he was close enough that she could feel him. Feel the warmth of his body seeping into her skin. Feel the vibrant energy that seemed to surround him.

"The flowers." She latched on to his question, using it as a lifeline to pull her out of the quagmire of sexual awareness that she was floundering in. "Dahlias are my favorites."

"Which ones are dahlias?"

Addy glanced at him, wondering if he was teasing, but he looked serious.

"The red, ruffled flowers in the terra-cotta pots beside the steps leading down onto the lawn. I take it you aren't all that interested in gardening?" she asked curiously.

Joe shrugged. "I like flowers, but I certainly haven't got the time to fool with them."

"Why not?"

Joe frowned at her as if she'd just asked a singularly stupid question. "Because I'm too busy, of course."

"There's no 'of course' about it. Gardening is a very relaxing hobby," Addy said earnestly. "It soothes the nerves and lowers the blood pressure."

"My blood pressure is just fine, and my nerves would soothe a lot quicker if people would just do as they're told!"

"Yes, but—"

"Allow me to point out another truism in dealing with a man," Joe said. "Don't try to change him until after you lock him up in marriage."

"I am not trying to change you!"

"That's what it sounds like from here."

"I was merely trying to help you to better health," she said to justify herself. "Physical exercise is important."

"If I wanted to grub around in the dirt, I'd have opted for farming," Joe said flatly, and Addy wisely let the subject drop. She still thought that Joe needed some form of physical exercise, but it was what he thought that was important.

"You have a lovely place here," she offered.

Joe glanced around the living room as if seeing it for the first time. "You think so?" His question caught her by surprise. "Maybe it's a feminine thing."

"What do you mean?"

"A woman designer decorated it, and the woman I was dating at the time loved it, too, but..." He gestured vaguely. "Somehow it's just..."

Addy nodded in sympathy. "Too perfect? It affects me that way too, but then I don't have to live in it. I can just admire it from afar."

"Tell me, if you were living in it, what would you do?"

Addy chuckled. "Mess it up a little. Drop some books on the end tables and knitting on the sofa. Put a bunch of family pictures on the grand piano."

Pictures? Joe considered her suggestion and felt a splinter of pain slice through him as he realized he didn't have any family pictures to put anywhere. His grandmother had died when he was too young to really remember her, and his mother had been so unhappy that she had always refused to let him take her picture.

But even if he didn't have any family pictures, he could display a friend-of-the-family picture, because Addy was his friend. He stared into her soft, brown eyes. He could take a snapshot of her and put it on the piano. Or, perhaps, put a full-length oil portrait of her over the mantel in place of that painting of dirty-white swirls that the decorator had assured him was such an excellent investment.

Or even better, he thought, his eyes narrowing consideringly, a nude painting of her. His whole body suddenly clenched as he had a vision of her pale, pink body reclining on a dark blue picnic blanket set in an ocean of green grass.

Golden sunlight was dappling her full breasts with alluring shadows and a gentle wind was causing their dusky tips to harden.

But he could hardly put a picture like that in the living room, he thought. Maybe in his study. No, he'd never get any work done. Maybe he could put it in his bedroom. Where it would probably disturb his sleep. There was no doubt about it, Addy was a very disturbing woman, even if she wasn't doing it consciously.

"Although the lack of knickknacks probably make it easier to clean," Addy offered placatingly when he continued to stare at her. Had she annoyed him by criticizing his home? But he had asked her for her opinion. And that was after he'd told her that she should answer questions she was asked. Addy swallowed a frustrated sigh. Relating to a man was no easy matter. Even one that she liked as much as she liked Joe. What it would be like with a complete stranger?

To Addy's relief, the phone rang, providing a distraction. Joe picked it up, identified himself, and then listened for a long moment.

"No!" His flat rejection of whatever the person at the other end had proposed was total and uncompromising. "He has my offer." Joe bit the words off. "He can take it or leave it."

Addy shuddered at Joe's implacable expression. If it were her, she'd just as soon leave it, she thought.

"I see no point in any further discussion. He can let my administrative assistant know what he's decided tomorrow." Joe slammed the phone down.

"Bad news?" Addy asked tentatively.

"That bastard went straight from me to a lawyer and had the lawyer call to try to get better terms."

"Which bastard are we talking about?"

"Edwards," Joe spat the word out as if it were a bad taste.

Addy frowned at him. "Wait a minute. You told me that

I should have a lawyer go over that contract you gave me, and yet you're damning David because he did exactly the same thing?"

"That's different," Joe insisted.

"I don't see how."

Joe stared at her in frustration. Why did she keep defending Edwards? He'd told her what the family had done to his mother. Could she possibly be attracted to Edwards? The very thought of her in Edwards's arms made him feel murderous.

"Does Edwards turn you on?" Joe asked harshly.

"Turn me on?" Addy repeated incredulously.

"Surely you've run across the concept before."

"How would I know if he turns me on?" she asked in confusion. "I only met the man for a few minutes this morning."

"He doesn't." Joe felt an overwhelming sense of relief chase through him.

"Why do you say that?" she asked, curious about how the male mind saw sexual attraction.

"Because you're either attracted to someone or you aren't. You should know that."

"Simply because a man doesn't turn me on when I first meet him doesn't mean that attraction won't grow," Addy said, hoping that it was true. It was really going to shorten her list of eligible men if it wasn't.

The melodious chimes of his doorbell interrupted a conversation that Addy was finding increasingly unsettling. Somehow, she didn't seem to be able to talk to Joe about sex in the abstract. Her body kept getting involved. And what was probably worse, her mind. The plain truth was that she found Joe fascinating, both mentally and physically. All she could hope was that it wouldn't last.

"Our food." Joe returned with a large boxed pizza and a carton of soda which he dumped on the coffee table.

Addy shuddered at the thought of what that greasy box was doing to the antique table's finish. She made a valiant effort not to interfere, which lasted for thirty seconds. Grabbing the box, she peered down at the surface. It looked unmarked.

"The pizza's big enough for two," Joe said dryly.

"I was worried about the surface of the table." She picked up a copy of the *Wall Street Journal* lying on the end table and carefully placed it on the table and then set the box back down.

"I distinctly remember warning you about trying to reform your victim before you've caught him."

Addy grimaced. "I know, I know, and I wouldn't do it with a stranger, but that's such a gorgeous piece."

"It's a table. It serves a function."

"Allow me to inform you, sir, that you are a Philistine."

"Your news flash is twenty years too late!" Joe snapped. "I've already been informed of my social shortcomings." He ripped a soda out of the six-pack and shoved it at her. "Do you want a drink?" he demanded.

Addy stared at him, taken aback by his reaction to what she'd meant as no more than gentle teasing. Why had he gotten so mad? Was it a male thing or was his reaction Joe's alone? Leery as she was to tackle anyone who looked that furious, she had to find out. If there were whole areas of conversation that were likely to produce unexpected anger in a man, she'd prefer to find out now. Not when she was dating a prospective husband.

"Yes, thank you." She automatically accepted the soft drink. "But what I'd really like to know is why my comment made you so mad."

"It did not make me mad!"

"You're still mad," Addy insisted. "And I need to know why. I didn't mean to make you angry. I was just teasing."

"By pointing out my social inadequacies?"

Addy winced at the bleakness darkening his eyes to navy. His pain made her feel cold inside. Cold and faintly panicked.

Carefully she set down her can of soda on the lid of the

box, trying to decide exactly what to say to repair the emotional damage she'd inadvertently caused.

"It's like whenever anyone makes a joke about fattening food or gaining weight and I cringe inside, assuming that the comment is aimed at me," she said slowly. "I might know that it isn't true in my mind, but in my heart I don't."

"What does your formerly fat state have to do with anything?" Joe demanded.

"A lot. I tend to make assumptions about what a person really means based on my own past experiences. I read things into their comments that they never meant. Like you just did. You took a harmless comment of mine and instilled all kinds of meaning in it that I never intended."

"Just drop it, will you?"

Addy took a deep breath. She didn't like conflict, but her gut instinct was to face this issue now. Because, if she didn't, it was going to lie between them and fester. It would poison their friendship, and she couldn't bear the thought of that happening.

"You promised to let me practice relating to men on you, and I want to practice. It's important to me to know why you reacted to my comment as you did."

Joe rubbed the back of his neck in frustration. Frustration at himself for having reacted so strongly and frustration at Addy for refusing to drop it. He was going to have to say something, that was certain. Addy had always been stubborn as hell. Should he tell her the truth? Inwardly, he cringed at the thought. He'd never told another soul about his one and only visit to his father when he'd been fourteen. It had been a soul-searing encounter. All the more so because in his childish daydreams Edwards had always welcomed him as his long-lost son.

The reality had been devastating. Edwards had looked at him as if he was less than human and had said that he didn't need to claim a Philistine for a son. That he already had a son. A son who knew what was expected of a gentleman.

And when Addy had used the word Philistine...

"Joe?"

Her soft voice tugged him out of his painful memories, and he looked up into her worried brown eyes. Even if Addy really thought that he was lacking socially she'd never be so unkind as to comment on it, he admitted. Addy didn't have a vicious bone in her body. She deserved the truth.

He took a deep breath and said, "I was fourteen when I finally pestered my mother into telling me who my father was. At that age, I was..." He shrugged. "Naive, I guess. I should have known that if Edwards had wanted to see me, he would have done so long before. I went to see him, expecting to be greeted with open arms and..."

"And he rejected you," Addy concluded. "He had to, of course, because if he didn't he would have also had to admit that he'd been wrong in ignoring you all those years. And from what I've heard about Andrew Edwards, he never admitted to being wrong about anything.

"What's more, it sounds as if people were only important to him for how he could use them. Since there was no way he could use you, he didn't want you around.

"He was not a nice man," Addy added, massively understating the case.

"No, he wasn't," Joe muttered, rather taken aback by her matter-of-fact analysis of what for him had been an emotionally devastating encounter. Somehow, it presented what had happened in a slightly different light.

Addy picked up a piece of pizza, took a bite and slowly chewed it as she considered the situation. "This could be a big problem in dating," she finally said. "What if I start to date a guy and accidentally activate whatever it is he feels inadequate about..."

"I don't feel inadequate!" Joe objected to her choice of words.

Addy ignored him. "And what's even worse, men seem to have some inborn rule against admitting a weakness."

"Presumably by the time you start delving into his psyche, you'll have been dating long enough that he won't totally withdraw."

"Perhaps," Addy said doubtfully. She had the disheartening feeling that finding a husband was going to be even harder than she'd originally thought.

"What movie are we going to watch?" she asked, to change the subject.

"There's a selection in that cabinet over there." He absently pointed to the large, carved armoire against the far wall. His attention was focused on watching her trying to catch a wayward strand of cheese with the tip of her pink tongue. An urge to press his mouth to hers surged through him, and he shifted restlessly, trying to think up some casual way to work in a kiss. He watched as she walked over to the cabinet, his attention riveted on the soft sway of her rounded hips beneath her worn denim jeans.

A suffocating sensation enveloped him at the thought of really kissing Addy. Properly kissing her. Thoroughly. Of following it through to its logical conclusion and having sex with her. A tremor of uncertainty shook him. He had the disquieting feeling that Addy would never just have sex with a man. She would make love to him. What would it be like to have Addy in love with him?

It would be a very bad idea. He immediately rejected the provocative thought. Women in love made demands on their lovers. They wanted commitments of time and emotion that he wasn't prepared to give. No, love was far too expensive a commodity for him. He couldn't afford it. Lust was easier to handle. And he had been honest with Addy. He'd told her straight out that he wasn't interested in marriage and the happily-ever-after bit.

And having been honest, there was no reason why they couldn't indulge in a little light lovemaking. In fact, he practically had an obligation to kiss her, he rationalized. It would give her something to measure those men she was intent on attracting against. A sense of anticipation filled him. First, he'd get her to sit next to him on the sofa and then he'd work on getting to actually touch her. Where? The provocative thought stifled his breathing. He was certainly spoiled for choice. Addy was a mass of eminently touchable parts.

"How about *The Name of the Rose?*" Addy looked over her shoulder at him.

"What about it?" Joe had trouble mentally shifting gears.

"I haven't had a chance to see it, and I like Eco."

"Fine by me. I haven't seen any of those movies. I just had the video store send me a selection."

"*The Rose* it is."

"Here." Joe got to his feet and took the film from her, sticking it into the VCR. "I'll start it."

Addy gave him the film and turned to study the seating facing the TV.

"Now what?" Joe asked, fearing that she was about to scuttle his half-formed plans before he even had a chance to try his luck.

"Logistics," she muttered. "I'm relatively certain that I should share the couch with a date—"

"Unless he has a communicable disease," Joe said dryly.

"Yes, but where on the couch do I sit?"

Joe stared at her in disbelief. "I can't believe you're making such a big deal out of this. Just sit."

"I know." She brightened. "I'll sit down before the man, and then where to sit will be his problem." She started toward the sofa only to have Joe sprint past her.

"Hey!" She grabbed for him and missed. "Stop messing up my plans."

Joe landed in the middle of the sofa, and Addy tripped over his feet falling across his lap. His hard thighs seemed to burn into her soft hips, and her face was pressed into the sleek fabric of his cotton shirt. An intoxicating aroma of soap and body warmth teased her nostrils.

Joe looked down into her face and felt a warm pleasure

engulf him at the luscious feel of her body pressed up against him—a pleasure mixed with a sense of confusion. He didn't know why he'd done that. He never indulged in silly games. Ever. And fighting over who got to sit down first was certainly silly, but he hadn't been able to resist. The serious expression on her face as she'd agonized over something as ridiculous as where to sit had been irresistible.

He swallowed as she wiggled in his lap and his body instinctively reacted. Somehow, with Addy, the normal rules didn't hold. Maybe because she didn't know about his reputation as a hardheaded businessman? With Addy he was free to be as juvenile as he liked. He didn't have to maintain any kind of front. He found the idea strangely intoxicating.

To his disappointment, Addy scooted off his lap and sat down beside him. Not quite as close as he would have preferred, but still close enough that he was devastatingly aware of her.

"Really!" Addy hoped she didn't sound as breathless as she felt. Being pressed up against him even for that short a time had played havoc with her self-control.

Joe grinned at her. "Yes, really. Now then shall we get down to the movie?"

"Good idea," she muttered, not liking the glint in his eyes. It promised devilment, and she wasn't sure what form it might take. Or that she'd be up to handling it. Or even if she'd want to, she conceded the truth. She liked touching Joe. And she was becoming increasingly obsessed with the idea of kissing him. Merely to see what it would be like. Not that there was anything worrisome with her curiosity, she rationalized. Most girls went through a fascination similar to what she was feeling in junior high school. She was just a late bloomer.

And since it was Joe who had activated her curiosity, she didn't have to worry about it being a complication once she actually started dating a potential husband. Because Joe was not husband material. For some reason the idea vaguely depressed her, and she determinedly shoved the thought to one side.

The sound of the movie starting distracted her and she gratefully turned to it. Her gratitude didn't last long. She shifted uneasily as she watched the prostitute begin to seduce the novitiate. It wasn't that she was offended. Nor did she consider the action gratuitous sex. The plain fact of the matter was that she found it very disconcerting to be watching the scene while sitting beside Joe. She wasn't sure exactly why, because both of them were adults and both of them had long since found out the facts of life. Imperceptibly, she began to edge away from him.

Joe turned and looked at her. "What's the matter?"

"Nothing," Addy muttered.

"Then why are you scuttling away from me?"

"I am not scuttling anywhere!"

He glanced from her to the view of the prostitute's bare breasts. "Are you a prude?"

"No!" She bit the word off.

"Good thing. Being a prude would be an almost insurmountable hindrance to marriage. But if you aren't a prude, what's wrong?"

"How about if we just forget it?" Addy glanced back at the screen, wincing when she was treated to a view of the prostitute's bare buttocks.

"No. I said I'd help you learn to date, and if you go to any movies you're bound to see naked bodies and sex. If you keep retreating, it's going to make the man wonder if you're a prude."

"Will you quit using that word? There is nothing wrong with me."

"You need to be desensitized," he said, "and the quickest way to do that is to dull whatever it is that's causing your embarrassment."

Addy stared at the small, white, pearlized button on his shirt while she frantically sifted through her memories for a sophisticated response. She didn't find a single applicable one. All she could think of was that she wanted him to kiss her, and she didn't want him to know how much she wanted it. Nor did she want him to find kissing her a disappointment. She couldn't bear for him to think that she was any less feminine than his normal girlfriends.

Just play it cool, she told herself as Joe's warm fingers grasped her neck and tilted her head up to his. She watched, mesmerized, as his face came closer and closer until it seemed to her muddled mind that his glittering eyes filled her whole field of vision. They were bright, sparkling with a promise of untold delights. Delights that drew her. Lured her closer to him despite the mass of uncertainties that filled her.

Longingly, Addy licked her lower lip, trying to control her erratic breathing. She could feel the heat from his body crowding against her. Engulfing her, tying her to him with sensual bonds. The faint scent of his cologne drifted into her lungs, coloring her thoughts. Giving them an erotic slant they'd never had before.

Her eyelids felt heavy, too heavy to keep up without an effort. An effort that was becoming harder and harder to maintain. She'd wanted to kiss him from the very first time she'd seen him sitting across that desk from her, she admitted honestly. She wanted to feel his lips against hers. Craved to discover what it would be like. Her body swayed toward him in unconscious invitation.

His large hands slipped to her shoulders, his warm fingertips digging into her skin as he pulled her closer. Involuntarily, Addy tensed as his lips softly brushed against hers and a skittering shower of sparks sizzled across her skin, disconcerting her. How could it feel like that? she wondered as his mouth finally closed roughly over hers.

His lips were warm. Warm and seeking as they pressed against her own. The skin on her face tightened as he rubbed his mouth back and forth against her lips. Despite the hectic flush she could feel burning across her cheekbones, she felt cold and she shivered convulsively, pressing closer to him.

His hand speared through her hair, holding her head still as he pressed against her mouth. A soft, yearning sound escaped her. She felt dizzy, totally disoriented and ravenously hungry.

She suddenly jerked as he ran the tip of his tongue over the line of her closed mouth. A tiny moan of pleasure escaped her and she instinctively opened her mouth.

Joe's reaction was immediate. He shoved his tongue inside her mouth with an obvious hunger that sent shivers of reaction cascading through her.

Addy clutched blindly at his broad shoulders, seeking a secure hold in a world that had suddenly lost all its normal anchors. The only reality for her was the feel of his mouth and her own reaction to it.

Addy twisted restlessly, trying to fit herself closer to the hard contours of his body, and then froze as she felt the heat of his hard fingers slip beneath the edge of her T-shirt to rest on her narrow rib cage.

His skin felt rough. Rough and hot and hard and infinitely exciting. Addy arched herself into his seeking hand and he rewarded her by slipping his hand up to cup one of her lace-covered breasts.

Addy trembled as a throbbing began to pound along her nerve endings, gathering in the pit of her stomach. She pressed closer as he rubbed his hand back and forth. She could feel her nipple convulsing beneath his ministrations and a strange sense of urgency wrapped its tentacles around her. An urgency that was inexorably pushing her toward some as yet unseeable goal.

But deep as her immersion in the sensations he was creating was, it wasn't strong enough to completely drown out the panicked sense of fear that trembled through her as she felt him begin to raise the hem of her shirt.

She couldn't let him see her body. The thought shattered her gossamer feelings of pleasure, ripping them to shreds.

Joe was used to making love to women who had as near to perfect bodies as there were. She couldn't begin to compare with that standard.

He'd be disgusted at the sight of her. The thought stilled her last lingering remnant of desire, and she mentally scrambled to find a way to retreat without sounding like either an outraged virgin or a tease.

"I am not a prude," she heard herself say in confusion. Why shouldn't she have said it? she thought wryly. Why shouldn't her mouth operate independently of her mind. Her body did.

"No," Joe said slowly as if he were having trouble focusing on her words. "Whatever else you might be, you most certainly aren't a prude." He shifted slightly, fitting her securely against his side and then turned back to the movie.

Whatever else she might be? Addy examined his words, wondering what he meant. Hadn't she responded to his kiss as she was supposed to? The chilling thought surfaced, but she refused to dwell on it. Joe knew that she had no experience at kissing men. She'd told him so herself. So he could hardly be surprised when she didn't show much technique. She'd learn, she thought, her eyes fixed longingly on his fingers, which such a short time ago had been creating havoc with her emotions. Given time and a little opportunity, she'd learn just fine. And the learning would be such fun. A euphoric sense of anticipation filled her.

Yes, Addy thought, relishing the pressure of Joe's body against her, Joe was a great teacher. She'd learn.

Five

"**M**anagement is out of their minds! This is a manufacturing plant, not some damn day nursery!" Ethel Lavinski, Joe's plant nurse, glared at Addy.

"I'll try not to get in your way," Addy forced a mild reply even though her impulse was to tell the woman exactly what she thought of her narrow ideas of what nursing should be. It would be much easier to accomplish her goals if she were on speaking terms with Ethel.

Ethel snorted. "No chance of that. I won't let you. You may be the latest hire, but I'm the one in charge of the infirmary."

Was the woman worried about her job? Addy wondered. Was that why she was being so unwelcoming? Addy moved to reassure her.

"Actually I'm not a hire. I'm a volunteer."

Ethel's mouth dropped open, and she stared at Addy in shock. "You actually mean to tell me that you aren't being paid?"

"That's what I mean to tell you."

"But why?" Ethel frowned in obvious confusion. "Unless…" Her expression hardened. "Are you doing this to try to show them what you can do?"

"Nope. I'm doing it because I've just gotten back from abroad, and I have time on my hands, and this job needs to be done."

Ethel shook her head, clearly unable to understand anyone being willing to work for free. "Better you than me. All those screaming kids throwing up all over the place. And worse," she added darkly.

"True," Addy agreed cheerfully. "But think of all the hugs and kisses I'll get."

Ethel scowled. "I get 'em, too and usually from the married ones. Never from anyone you'd welcome a kiss from. Like the boss."

"Oh?" Addy murmured encouragingly, curious about how his employees saw Joe.

"Yeah, worse luck. He never fools around at work. Not that he has to." Ethel rolled her eyes. "One afternoon last summer I caught a glimpse of the woman he was dating when she came to pick him up. She was tall, blond, impossibly slim and wearing an outfit to kill for. The kind of woman you hate on sight."

Maybe fat people weren't the only ones who had problems with how people saw them, Addy thought.

"Well, since you're here, you can use that desk." Ethel gestured toward a large, gray-metal desk shoved into a corner of her office. "What else you want?"

"An examining room and a room big enough to hold classes in," Addy replied promptly.

Ethel frowned thoughtfully. "There are three examining rooms and I can only use one at a time, so that won't be a problem. As for a meeting room… There's an empty storeroom at the end of the hall you can have. Come on, I'll show you."

Addy followed her down a short hallway and looked

through the door Ethel threw open with a critical eye. The room was big enough, but the institutional gray walls were very off-putting.

"Paint," Addy muttered. "Bright paint and lots of posters."

"I don't know about that," Ethel said doubtfully. "Maintenance only seems to operate in neutrals."

"Stuff maintenance! Surroundings are very important to a patient's mental health."

Ethel eyed Addy in resignation. "I don't know why I always get the wide-eyed idealists dumped on me. Just once I'd like to get a cynic. I mean, it's not like you're some kid fresh out of nursing school. You're old enough to know better."

Addy laughed. "Maybe I've just got a bad case of arrested development."

"It's no laughing matter," Ethel insisted. "Just you remember that I'm not going to get involved. I do my job and I draw my pay and that's it."

"I'll remember," Addy promised, wondering what made Ethel so negative. She couldn't be much more than forty and she looked to be in good health. Perhaps she had had a blighted love affair?

"You decide what colors you want, and I'll ask maintenance to get them for you. Not that I think much of your chances of getting them."

"Thanks, and I appreciate your showing me around," Addy said.

"I did it because personnel told me to cooperate with you," Ethel said flatly.

"Whatever. I still appreciate it. Bye."

Addy pushed open the door that led to the front of the building and escaped. She paused as she reached the corridor that led to Joe's office, checking her watch. It was two-thirty. She had time to stop and say hello.

A spurt of excitement twisted through her, the strength of which was enough to set off alarm bells in her mind.

Maybe it wasn't a good idea for her to give in to her growing compulsion to be around Joe. To talk to him. To simply look at him. To remember what it had been like to kiss him. She shivered as her mind obligingly recalled the exact feel and taste and texture of his mouth.

Maybe her intense reaction was just because Joe was the first man that she had ever really kissed, she considered. Maybe her hormones were simply reacting to kissing a very attractive man. Maybe she would have reacted the same if any attractive man had kissed her?

Addy took a deep breath, trying not to worry about it. She had plenty of other things to worry about. Such as the Wheelings' party this evening. Her stomach did a nervous flip-flop. Despite the fact that she knew Joe was right about using the party as an opportunity to view the competition, she still had a bad feeling about the whole thing. Social catastrophes seemed to attach themselves to her without any effort on her part.

Joe would be with her, she told herself, trying to soothe her fears. And she had a new dress to wear. She'd driven down to Philadelphia yesterday and bought the most gorgeous dress she'd ever seen. And in forty minutes, the hair stylist Kathy had recommended was going to work magic on her sedate hairstyle. At least, Addy hoped so. She was feeling nervous enough about the party tonight without the added handicap of knowing that her hair was hopelessly out of style.

Determinedly resisting the impulse to stop by Joe's office, Addy headed toward the parking lot.

A male voice caught her attention as she emerged from the building. "Good morning."

Addy turned toward the voice, squinting in the brilliant sunlight in an effort to see better.

David Edwards. She recognized the face. Instinctively she studied his blunt features, looking for some resemblance to Joe, but she couldn't find any.

"I'm David Edwards, Miss Edson," he said, assuming

her abstracted expression was caused by a failure to recognize him. He held out his hand.

Addy automatically took it and his fingers closed around
her slight hand firmly. Curiously, she analyzed her reaction
to his touch. She found it warm, firm and totally neutral.
She might as well have been shaking the hand of the eighty-
year-old nun who'd kept records for her at the clinic in
Africa. Why was her reaction to Joe so different? Addy
worried the question around in her mind. Why did one man
make her feel as if she'd been shoved down a fifty-foot
slide blindfolded, and the other got no reaction whatsoever?

"I have caught you at a bad time, haven't I?" David
said ruefully.

"No," Addy hastily disclaimed. "I was just thinking."

"Happy thoughts, I hope."

Addy swallowed, realizing that she could hardly say
what she'd really been thinking, so that meant she had to
say something else. Men expected you to contribute to the
conversation. Desperately she searched for a subject. The
clinic. She suddenly remembered why she was there in the
first place.

"I'm organizing a baby clinic for the children of the
company's employees, and I was looking over the facilities
available," Addy offered and then relaxed slightly as she
waited for him to add something to the conversation.

David lifted his brown eyebrows in surprise. "How for-
ward-thinking of Barrington. Somehow, I wouldn't have
thought that he would be all that concerned about his employees."

Addy lost her reticence in her defense of Joe. "He is
very concerned about his employees' well-being."

"If you say so. Maybe it's because I haven't seen much
of his softer side. He reminds me of my father. In one of
his more autocratic moods," David added wryly.

Addy didn't know what to say. She didn't want to admit
that she knew about David's dealings with Joe. That admission might lead to questions that she didn't want to

answer. And she certainly didn't want to pursue the subject of any resemblance between Joe and Andrew Edwards. That secret wasn't hers to tell. Addy stifled a sigh. Conversation between the sexes was no easy matter.

"Or am I missing something?" David's eyes suddenly narrowed. "Are you and Barrington involved?"

"Not the way I think you mean it." Addy ignored the wistful pang she felt at the admission. "Joe is a very good friend from my childhood, and he's helping me get resettled."

David grinned at her. "I hope he didn't unsettle you in the first place."

Addy smiled back. "I just got back from four years in Africa."

"So you're a returning exile, too. You'll have to come out to dinner with me one evening, and we can compare notes on how the old town has changed."

Addy blinked, unsure of what to say. She didn't feel that she'd learned anywhere near enough from Joe to start dating on her own. Added to which, she was positive that he would view her dating David as an act of betrayal, and she wasn't willing to hurt Joe.

Mentally, she searched through her memories of old movies, searching for a graceful way to turn down a date. "Maybe when I've gotten settled," she murmured.

"I'll give you a call next week. Is your phone number listed?"

"Yes." Addy felt an overwhelming sense of relief at having managed to postpone the problem of what to do about David.

"Till later, then." With a smile, David continued into the offices, and Addy hurried to her hairstyling appointment.

The hairstylist turned out to be every bit as good as Kathy had claimed, and Addy was ecstatic at her new style. Her wave of euphoria didn't begin to ebb until Joe arrived to take her to the party.

What was wrong? she wondered nervously as Joe stood on her doorstep and stared at her. She loved the way her hair swirled around her neck when she swung her head, but maybe the style was too young for her? Or maybe it was her dress? The soft, coppery-bronze silk was far more sophisticated than anything she'd ever owned. Addy, who normally picked her clothes with the intention of avoiding attention, not attracting it, had allowed herself to be guided by the saleswoman's obvious chic. Had it had been a mistake?

"Do I look okay?" Addy finally asked.

Okay? Joe's eyes wandered over the mass of red curls that tumbled to her shoulders. His gaze drifted lower, down over the glittery silk material of her dress, which lovingly molded her rounded curves. His fingers twitched with a compulsive urge to touch those curves again, this time without any barrier between them. He wanted to run his fingers through the soft strands of her hair. To bury his face in her curls and inhale the flowery scent that she was wearing. He wanted to caress the swell of her breasts, exposed by the deep cut of her neckline, with his mouth. "Okay" didn't begin to describe his reaction to how she looked.

And the reaction every other man at the party would have to her. Every man there was going to want to touch her and kiss her just as he did. And Addy wasn't ready yet to fend them off, he told himself, rationalizing the dismay he felt at the idea. There was still too much that he had to teach her before she was ready to go out in the real world.

"I could change into something else?"

Her tentative voice broke into his confused thoughts, and he raised his eyes to hers. They were filled with uncertainty. An uncertainty that roused his protective feelings. Addy didn't have a great deal of self-confidence and if he asked her to change—even if it was for her own good—she'd be crushed. And it wasn't as if she was going alone, he reassured himself. He'd be there to protect her if anyone got out of line.

"Please don't," he said. "You look spectacular."

"Oh?" Addy blinked uncertainly at his husky tone. Could he really think she looked great or was he merely trying to make her feel better?

"First lesson of the night," Joe said. "When your escort compliments you, smile and say thank you."

"Sorry. It's just that I haven't had all that many compliments come my way. I guess I'm always looking for the hidden meaning behind the surface remark."

"Addy, I promise you, when I want to say something, I'll say it. You don't have to wonder what I really mean."

Addy smiled at him, and Joe felt a jolt of desire rock him. Lord, did she have even the faintest idea just how potent her smile was? It made a man want to kiss her luscious lips. To absorb her smile with his own mouth.

"You look pretty good yourself." She glanced approvingly at his tailored gray suit. Her eyes slipped downwards to linger on the flatness of his belly. She hurriedly caught herself as her gaze began to drift lower. What was the matter with her? All but drooling over him. This was Joe. Her old friend.

Joe used her words as an excuse to touch her.

"Now, on the second date, if you still like the guy, you can greet him with a little more than a compliment."

He put his arms around her and gently pulled her up against him. He could feel the fragile bones of her rib cage through the thin silk of her dress, and his eyes widened as he realized that what he couldn't feel was underwear. She wasn't wearing a bra! All that was between him and her luscious breasts was a thin layer of soft silk.

No, don't think about it, he ordered himself, trying to concentrate on one thing at a time.

Lowering his head, he unerringly found her mouth, intending to give her a casual kiss, but his intentions shattered when his mouth covered hers. All he could think of was the feel of her nestled in his arms. Of the heady taste of her warm lips. He needed this, he thought hazily. He needed it to sustain him through what he was beginning to think would be an even more trying night than he'd originally thought. He lightly ran the tip of his tongue along her lower lip.

Addy responded by opening her mouth, and his thoughts were drowned in the flood of need that shook him. His arms tightened, crushing her soft breasts into his chest, and his tongue surged into her mouth, stroking over her tongue.

The soft yearning sound Addy made deep in her throat burned along his nerve endings. More, he thought foggily. He wanted more. His hand plunged into the silken mass of her curls, holding her head steady as his lips wandered across her cheek. The faint, flowery smell of her captivated him, and he nuzzled the soft skin beneath her ear. His guts clenched in longing as she trembled in his arms, and he lightly bit her tender earlobe, tasting her exquisite flesh.

Addy tasted so good. Sweet, and heavy with the promise of untold delights. Better than he could ever remember a woman tasting. His lips wandered back over her face, pausing to brush over the feathery softness of her eyelashes. He felt them quiver and a sense of power shook him. He felt omnipotent.

It was the almost painful tightness of his body that finally recalled him to what he was doing. He had to stop, and stop now, or he wouldn't be able to. He was perilously close to losing what little control he still had. He forced himself to drop his arms and step away from her.

Addy ran the tongue over her throbbing lips and blinked, trying to bring the world into focus again. It took several seconds.

"That is the normal way to greet someone you're dating." Joe tried to lighten the tension palpably vibrating in the air between them.

If that was the way you kissed someone you were only dating, how did you go about kissing a lover? The provocative thought flitted through her mind, doing nothing to help her composure. Making a supreme effort to sound normal, she said, "Would you like something to drink before we go?"

"What do you have?"

"Um, actually just diet soda."

"Then why did you offer me a drink?"

Because your kiss addled my thought processes, she thought ruefully. "Because every movie I've ever seen the woman always asks the man if he wants a drink," she substituted. "It seemed like the thing to do."

Joe laughed—a warm, rich sound that helped to restore her sense of equilibrium.

"Things could get interesting if you intend to copy movie behavior."

Addy flushed, remembering the behavior of the only female in the only movie they'd watched. She determinedly changed the subject. "What kind of a day did you have?"

"Is that the second thing women ask men in movies?"

"No, it's the thing a woman asks a man who looks as tired as you do." Her eyes lingered on the deeply carved lines beside his mouth.

Joe stretched, and the material of his jacket pulled tightly across his shoulders, emphasizing their breath to the avidly watching Addy. "I am tired," he admitted. "It was a long day, but a satisfying one for all that. We landed a big contract to supply the components for a new computer a company in Eastern Europe is developing. We may have to expand even more than I'd originally thought we would. And Edwards came by today."

Addy shivered as Joe's face suddenly hardened into predatory lines. He looked absolutely ruthless.

"Yes, I saw him when I was out at the plant this afternoon," Addy said carefully. She wasn't sure if she should mention seeing David or not, but if she didn't and Joe somehow found out, he might think that she was trying to hide it from him. Addy stifled a sigh. Joe might be a very intelligent man, but about David Edwards he was plain stupid.

Joe frowned. "You were out at the plant this afternoon?"

Addy nodded. "I wanted to see what facilities the nursing unit had for me to use. When I was leaving, I ran into David, who was on his way in. He stopped to say hello."

"I imagine he does it very well," Joe sneered. "With his background."

"In what?" Addy said dryly. "Politeness?"

"In society."

"David Edwards seems like a pretty average guy to me when it comes to manners."

"We're going to be late." Joe abruptly changed the subject, and Addy let him do it. Joe had hated David Edwards his entire life. Hated and, she rather suspected, envied him, although Joe would never admit it. Probably not even to himself. He wasn't suddenly about to change because of something she said. If he ever did change his mind, it would have to be a gradual process of learning to see David as a person in his own right and not as an extension of their mutual father.

She followed Joe out to the car and tried to ignore the oppressive silence that filled it on the short drive to the Wheelings' house.

Addy's eyes widened as they pulled up in front of a long, low modern house from which the sounds of a party in full swing were emanating. She swallowed nervously as she watched a gorgeous woman climb out of the car in front of them and head toward the door with her date.

"Don't worry." Joe's annoyance at her championship of Edwards dissolved at her worried expression. "That's just Cindy Laukin. She's no competition for you."

"Partiality is all well and good, but you need glasses. That woman looks spectacular."

"True." Joe opened the car door for her. "But you want to get married, and Cindy's not the kind of woman any man with an ounce of self-preservation would marry."

Addy looked back at the woman, who was laughing uproariously at something the man beside her had said.

"Why not?" she asked curiously.

"Because Cindy will sleep with anyone who is willing to show her a good time and in this day and age promiscuity is damn dangerous."

Addy grimaced. "It's a sad commentary on mankind that fear will do what ethics can't."

Joe shrugged. "Take it up with Mother Nature, not me. I've never fooled around with Cindy."

The knowledge made her feel fractionally better. This party was going to be hard enough to get through without having to deal with Joe's ex-lovers.

"Joe! You were able to come after all." As they entered the house, their hostess enveloped Joe in a hug that Addy thought was far more enthusiastic than the occasion warranted.

"Cookie." Joe deftly extricated himself. "You remember Addy Edson, don't you?"

"I don't think..." Addy watched with a satisfaction that her mind told her was childish, but her emotions positively relished, as Cookie's mouth rounded to a surprised O when she finally placed her. "But you used to be so fat."

"And you used to be so thin." Addy didn't realize she'd said the words aloud until Joe choked.

Cookie looked at her in shock, and Addy stifled a sigh. This evening was going to be a disaster. She knew it. She hadn't been here five minutes and she'd already insulted her hostess.

To her surprise, Cookie didn't react as she'd expected. "Sorry, Addy. That just slipped out. I didn't mean to be bitchy. At least, not that bitchy."

"S'okay." Addy was more than willing to meet her halfway.

"Later on, when the party has settled down a little, you'll have to tell me what you've been doing all these years."

"Love to," Addy lied, making her escape as another couple came up the walk.

Addy unconsciously inched closer to Joe as the noise of

the party hit her the minute they were inside. She could feel that old familiar feeling of social inadequacy freezing her mind. Her smile felt pasted on, and her stomach was beginning to twist nervously.

"From the expression on your face, you must be expecting a serial killer to jump you. This group is basically harmless. Come on, let's practice mingling."

Reminding herself that was why she was there, Addy trailed along behind Joe as he slowly made his way through the crowd, stopping along the way to introduce her to various people. At each introduction, Addy forced a smile, trying to remember who everyone was, but she couldn't. There were simply too many of them.

"Joe Barrington, just the man I want to see. I need something."

Addy turned at the sound of a husky, female voice. She watched as a well-dressed woman of about thirty stood on tiptoe to plant a kiss on Joe's cheek.

"Hi, there." She smiled warmly at Addy. "I'm Barbara Kelvington. Are you one of Joe's friends from New York?"

"Her name is Addy Edson, and she's local," Joe said, leaving Addy wondering why he didn't deny that she was a friend. At least the kind of a friend that she was sure Barbara had in mind.

"I just returned from overseas," Addy explained. "I was born here in Hamilton."

Barbara grimaced. "You and everyone else. I swear, sometimes I feel like the only person who ever moved into this town."

"Barbara's husband is a local minister," Joe told Addy. "Barbara is an artist."

"I try, but in the art world you have to die first to get discovered."

Addy chuckled. "You could try cutting off your ear."

Barbara shook her head mournfully. "My husband's congregation wouldn't like it. They still haven't gotten over my painting nudes."

"What was it you wanted, Barbara?" Joe asked.

"Dan Zeving lost his job and his wife is frantic with worry. I was hoping that you'd give him a job."

"No." Joe's flat refusal caught Addy by surprise, even though Barbara didn't seem all that shocked.

Barbara sighed. "Well, if you should change your mind…"

"I won't."

"It was nice to meet you, Addy."

"Goodbye." Addy waited until Barbara had moved out of hearing and then asked Joe, "Why won't you give him a job?"

"Because I've got too much sense."

"Charity has nothing to do with sense," Addy insisted. "It has to do with compassion and…"

"Spare me the bleeding-heart liberal dogma."

Addy glared at him. "Spare me the convenient labels! You could help."

"Zeving is addicted to cocaine. He's lost two jobs for being high at work, and at the moment he's out on bail for vehicular manslaughter. He got high and drove headfirst into a car full of teenagers. Killed two of them," Joe said flatly.

"Maybe if he were to get treatment…"

"He's been in and out of treatment centers for years."

"Well, if he won't help himself, there isn't a great deal anyone can do for him. But…" She frowned thoughtfully off into the distance as she considered the problem.

"Could you find a job for his wife?" she finally asked.

"What?"

"Well, Barbara said Zeving's wife was worried, presumably about getting money to pay the bills. If you gave her a job, she could provide for herself until her husband gets his act together."

Joe stared down into her pleading eyes and knew he was going to agree, even though he didn't want anything to do with drugs. Even secondhand.

"How about if I give Barbara a check for the wife?"

"Absolutely not! A job means that the woman can take control of her own life. Living on handouts, even well-meant ones, would destroy her self-esteem."

Joe gave up. "All right. I'll offer her a job. But whether she takes it or not is strictly up to her."

"More than fair." Addy beamed at him and Joe felt a warmth envelop him at her approval. She wasn't as hopelessly idealistic as he'd originally thought. She might be a reformer, but her reforming was strongly allied to common sense. He felt a tremor of unease. In the long run, that might turn out to be far more dangerous.

Six

"**O**h, look, they have a Ping-Pong table." Addy pointed toward an alcove in the Wheelers' huge family room.

"Hmm," Joe muttered, keeping a wary eye on a strange-looking woman who had been stalking him for the last ten minutes. She noticed his interest, misinterpreted the reason, and gave him a wide smile.

"Let's play a game," Joe hurriedly said. There was no way the woman could pester him if he were playing. From the determined look on her face, nothing short of brutal frankness would get rid of her. That was something he didn't want to be forced into, because it would be bound to upset Addy, and she was already nervous enough.

"Play?" Addy glanced from the empty table to him. "You want to play?"

"Unless you're chicken?" Joe goaded as the woman got closer.

Addy gave him a seraphic smile that he immediately mistrusted, but not as much as he mistrusted the approaching woman.

"Come on." He took Addy's arm and hustled her over to the table. "I'll take it easy on you."

"You're all heart," Addy said demurely. Take it easy on her indeed! What Joe needed was a sharp lesson in the dangers of underestimating a woman. She picked up a paddle and tested its balance.

"You serve," she said.

Joe, with a cautious look over his shoulder for the woman's whereabouts, lobbed the ball over the net. It came back at him before he even got his paddle up to return it. He blinked in surprise.

"My serve," Addy said.

Joe tightened his grip on the paddle and waited for her serve. The ball whizzed by him so fast he was only able to get off a feeble swipe at it.

He frowned at the impossibly innocent-looking Addy.

"My point," she announced.

Joe tensed in preparation, watching her movement. As a result he was able to get his paddle on the ball, not that it did him any good. His return went wild, landing off the table.

Addy rescued the ball, smiled at him and said, "Ready?"

Joe waited, determined not to be beaten at something as simple as Ping-Pong. He missed again.

When the score was fifteen to nothing, he managed to return the ball twice before she was able to score. Flushed with a sense of accomplishment, he rocked back on his heels and bumped into someone. He turned to apologize and found the woman.

"Oh, I'm so sorry!" Her breathless voice was cloying. As if each word were dripping saccharin.

"S'okay," Joe muttered, turning back to Addy.

The woman didn't take the hint. "I'm Sally Kittering. I've been admiring your game," she said to Addy. "You have such a...masculine approach to the game."

"How can you say that? I'm winning," Addy shot back, and then glanced around as her words were greeted with a chuckle from someone standing behind her. A slow flush crawled up over her skin as she realized that they'd attracted an audience. She had been so busy wiping up the floor with Joe she hadn't even noticed. She winced. She might not know much about dating, but even she knew that you weren't supposed to show a man up at sports.

"I know!" Sally clapped her hands in an affected gesture that set Joe's teeth on edge. Picking up a spare paddle, she inched closer to Joe. "I'll help you."

Addy hurriedly sent the ball over the net at only a small fraction of its normal speed. With Sally's advent on the scene, the game had lost all its fun and Addy only wanted to get it over with. She hadn't meant to beat Joe like that. Well, actually, she had, she admitted honestly as she weakly swiped at the ball and let it go off the table. She just hadn't wanted an audience while she did it.

Joe glanced sharply at Addy as he served, no easy task with Sally practically hanging on his arm.

Addy returned it long, letting Joe score the point.

"Oh!" the woman squealed, and Joe winced at the sound. "I'm bringing you good luck. That's two in a row we've scored."

"And I think I'll quit while I'm ahead." Joe set his paddle down on the table and, taking Addy's arm, marched her away.

Addy stole a quick glance at his tightly compressed lips and her heart sank. He was mad because she'd beaten him in front of everyone. Not just beaten, she admitted, she'd humiliated him.

"Don't you ever do anything like that again!" Joe snapped once they'd reached the relative privacy of the garden. "I felt like a fool."

"I'm sorry," Addy apologized. "I wasn't thinking about how a date would feel about getting his brains beat out."

He frowned at her. "What are you talking about?"

"About beating you."

"I didn't mind that. You beat me fairly. What I minded was at the end when you quit playing and let me win. I find that patronizing."

Addy blinked, taken aback by what had actually annoyed him. Although perhaps she shouldn't have been. Joe was a very competitive person, but he wasn't the least bit petty.

"Where on earth did you learn to play like that?" he asked.

"In Africa, from a pair of Chinese revolutionaries."

"What!"

Addy nodded. "At least, we thought they were. Han and Fu just appeared one day, claiming to be students, but they never seemed to study anything. They spent their time preaching revolution and the wonders of communism to the local people."

"And in their spare time they taught you to play table tennis as a blood sport?"

"Well, you can't foment revolution all the time. It started when they used to come over to the clinic and try to convert us."

"Convert a bunch of nuns to communism?"

"Actually, their contention was that the nuns were already communists because they didn't own anything personally, and they all worked for the greater good with very little personal reward."

"There's a certain amount of truth to that," Joe conceded. "But there's a big difference between communism and Marxism."

"Anyway, once they tasted Sister Ave's brownies they were hooked. They started coming for supper and staying to pass the evening. That's when they taught me to play table tennis."

"It must be true that God looks after fools. They could have killed you!"

"Nonsense. Han and Fu wouldn't have hurt us. They

needed us to patch them up whenever they ran afoul of the local warring tribal factions.''

Joe shook his head, not wanting to hear any more. He was going to have nightmares about what might have happened to her already.

Addy looked around as a particularly loud burst of laughter caught her attention. Everyone at the party seemed to be having a wonderful time, so why wasn't she? And what was worse, she wasn't getting much practice in talking to people. With Joe at her side, everyone concentrated their conversation on him. The most she received was a few occasional, well-mannered crumbs, which was doing nothing to advance her goal.

She spoke her thoughts aloud. "I should try to circulate by myself for a while."

"You aren't ready yet," Joe said.

"True," Addy conceded, "but I need the practice. How about if I walk slowly over to the refreshment table and see what happens?"

"I don't like it."

"I don't like it, either, but I need to try. Maybe someone will talk to me, and I can practice on them."

"But—"

"And if I need help, I can always find you."

"All right." Joe gave in. "But don't you dare wander off with anyone."

"I won't," Addy assured him, meaning it. Taking a deep breath, she headed toward the end of the refreshment table where a pudgy man was loading prawns on his plate.

The man interpreted her nervous hello as an invitation to tell her his life story. By the time Addy was able to escape almost an hour later, she knew far more about Ed than she wanted to.

Deciding that she needed a few minutes alone to catch her breath and psych herself up to approach someone else, she made her way back to the bathhouse at the far end of the swimming pool. To her relief, it was deserted.

She inched into the shadows beside the bathhouse and watched the milling crowd around the edge of the swimming pool. Even though she knew that she should be out there with them, practicing her social skills, she couldn't quite make herself move. All she wanted to do was to hide. Hide from both the noise and the strain of trying to hold up her end of the conversation.

She carefully scanned the area looking for Joe, finally locating him standing by the open patio door to the house. A well dressed brunette was leaning toward him, gesturing emphatically with her hand. Joe was listening to her with a curiously blank expression that Addy couldn't read.

It was no wonder Joe was a cynic, if tonight was a typical example of how people treated him, Addy thought as she continued to watch him. During the time that Joe had kept her by his side, she'd lost count of the number of people who had asked him for something. Their requests had ranged from barely disguised begging to trying to interest him in a business investment. Even the minister's wife, who had seemed to like Joe, had wanted something. The fact that it wasn't for herself didn't really make any difference. Barbara had still wanted something.

Addy watched in growing annoyance as the brunette put her hand on the lapel of Joe's jacket, like a predator afraid that her quarry might bolt. The woman wanted something from him, too. That much was clear. Addy took a gulp of her iced tea. The woman wanted his body.

So did she, Addy admitted in a burst of honesty. She wanted to take his clothes off and explore the shape and texture of his body. She wanted to feel the muscles moving beneath his warm, supple skin. She wanted to feel the strength of his arms around her, holding her tightly against him. She wanted to feel his lips moving over her body. She wanted to follow the explosive feelings he'd already ignited with his kisses through to their conclusion.

She wanted to make love to Joe. Addy squarely faced the fact. Even knowing that there was no future in it, she still wanted to do it. She took a deep, steadying breath and tried to think.

Okay, so you're attracted to Joe in a big way. She allowed the words to form in her mind. So what? There was no harm in her attraction. Nor was it likely she'd have the opportunity to do anything about it. Common sense told her that he was hardly likely to want her when gorgeous, self-assured women like the brunette were falling all over themselves to get into his bed. Besides, she doubted if she'd have the courage to expose her body to his knowledgeable eyes. She might not be fat anymore, but her body still carried the scars of when she had been.

"Well, hello there. Where have you been all my life?" A man's smooth, self-satisfied voice grated on Addy's nerves and her first impulse was to run. She was tired, and her nerves were frayed with the effort she'd expended at being social. She simply didn't feel up to searching frantically for suitable rejoinders to what passed for conversation among this group.

Then, reminding herself that any experience interacting with men would be valuable, Addy pasted a smile on her face.

"You must be new in town." The man oozed closer to her, and Addy instinctively inched back, only to find her retreat blocked by the bathhouse behind her. "I know I'd remember if I'd met you before." His eyes wandered blatantly down over her body, and Addy felt a shimmer of distaste.

"I'm Warren White." He held out his hand.

Captive to the social conventions, Addy took it despite a deep disinclination to touch him, and muttered, "Addy Edson."

"And where did you spring from, Addy?" His fingers tightened around hers.

He obviously needed a lesson in basic biology, Addy thought tartly, but she lacked the self-confidence to say it aloud. Instead, she murmured, "I was born here."

"And I've never met you!" His eyebrows rose in mock horror. "Fortunately, we can remedy that. Why don't you come into the study, and you can tell me all about yourself?"

Said the spider to the fly, Addy thought. "It's much too nice an evening to go inside," she said, scrambling for an excuse. She might not have much experience with men, but a two-year-old could tell that it would be a very bad idea to go anywhere out of the public eye with this guy.

Warren's full mouth momentarily tightened in annoyance, and then he forced a smile that looked artificial. "As you wish. We can talk right here."

He put his hand on the wall beside her shoulder and leaned forward, effectively shutting her off from the rest of the party.

Addy swallowed uneasily. There might be no logical reason for it, but she felt threatened. She wanted Warren to move back, but she lacked the social expertise to ask him to do it gracefully and the thought of creating a scene was untenable. She took a deep breath, reminded herself of her goals and prepared to endure.

"If you're from right around here, how come I never met you?" he repeated.

"I've just returned from four years in Africa," Addy offered as her contribution to the conversation.

"Africa! I've always wanted to go big-game hunting there. I've hunted most of the things around here. Did you get in any hunting?"

"No, I got my food from the store like most Africans," Addy said, anger at his desire to go and kill something momentarily overriding her sense of shyness.

To her surprise, Warren seemed to think she was making a joke. He began to laugh uproariously. "A sense of humor, too," he chortled. "I like that in a woman. My ex-wife had absolutely no sense of humor."

Addy very much suspected that having him for a husband would be enough to dampen the most ebullient spirit.

"But I finally got rid of her. The divorce was final this week." His expression was a strange blend of glee, anticipation and dread. "That's why Cookie's having this party. To get me back in the social swim. You aren't married, are you?" He glanced around as if expecting to find a husband lurking in the shrubbery.

"No."

"Good." He gave her a satisfied smile. "Usually the lookers are. The only ones that seemed to be unmarried these days are the losers."

"I've noticed that," Addy murmured, but Warren's colossal self-conceit didn't allow him to see anything personal in her comment.

"And the few who aren't losers are all busy falling over themselves to impress the local bastard made good." Warren gestured toward Joe, and Addy felt a flash of rage that made her want to smack him. Hard.

"Money!" Warren snorted in disgust. "If you've got enough of it, nothing else matters."

"Don't you have enough?" Anger fueled Addy's comment.

Warren blinked, peering closer at Addy as if trying decide if she were being insulting or merely trying to find out more about him.

"Don't you worry your little head about it," he finally said. "Even with the outrageous support payments the judge gave my wife for the kids, I've got enough to show you a good time."

Addy stared at Warren in frustration. She couldn't even manage to insult a man with any degree of success.

Her frustration turned to revulsion as he inched closer. She could feel the heat from his body as he crowded up against her, threatening both her sense of personal safety and her natural fastidiousness. Nervously, she glanced around, looking for a graceful way out.

"Don't worry. No one can see us." Warren misunderstood her agitation. "I just want to show you that the best times don't take any money." He swooped down toward her mouth, and Addy jerked sideways. His lips landed on her shoulder at the base of her neck, and she could feel his hot mouth greedily fastening on to her skin like a leech.

A sense of panic engulfed her. She wanted out. Now! And to hell with what anyone thought. Having his mouth on her was a violation. She put her hands against his chest and pushed. To no avail. Warren might be a self-centered egotist, but he was a well-conditioned, self-centered egotist.

"Oh, lady, you are one hot number." Warren's thickening voice increased Addy's fear. "Let's ditch this crowd and go back to my place."

"No, thank you." Addy tried to inch away from him.

His hand came up and brushed over her breast.

"Don't!" Addy spit out.

"You don't have to play coy with me," Warren muttered. "I'll make it good for you."

"Take your hands off her while you can still operate them!"

Addy sagged against the building in relief at the harsh sound of Joe's voice.

Warren jerked around and glared at him. "Hell, man, you haven't got a monopoly on all the attractive women! Go back to your lady lawyer."

"Move!" Joe emphasized his command by grabbing the collar of Warren's shirt and jerking him away from Addy.

"It's all right, Joe," Addy said, trying to defuse Joe's anger. The muscles along his jaw were bunched into thick cords, and his lips were firmly clamped together. He looked absolutely murderous.

That fact suddenly seemed to filter through Warren's self-confidence. He hastily stepped back several paces.

"Cookie would never forgive me if I beat up one of her guests," he threw at Addy, all the while keeping a cautious eye on Joe.

"True," Addy agreed, willing him to go.

"I'll give you a call," Warren told her as he finally left.

Addy let out her breath in a long, shuddering sigh and instinctively moved toward Joe. His arms closed comfortingly around her, and she pressed her cheek against his chest. The silky smoothness of his tie caressed her flushed cheek and the warm, musky scent of his body drifted into her lungs, replacing the blatantly aggressive cologne Warren had been wearing. A feeling of safety began to loosen her tight muscles and soothe her jagged nerves.

"Thanks, Joe," she muttered. "I couldn't seem to convince him that I didn't want to play whatever game he had in mind. I tell you, I'm beginning to get discouraged about my chances of ever finding a husband."

Joe gave her a comforting squeeze and dropped a kiss on the top of her head. "It's the early days of your campaign and, besides, I very much doubt that you're ever going to be a match for Warren White."

"It wasn't just him, although he certainly took the prize for sheer obnoxiousness." Addy reluctantly stepped back. It was not a good idea for her to get into the habit of using Joe as an emotional prop. It wasn't fair to him, and it was downright dangerous to her own peace of mind.

"It was the whole thing," she said slowly. "No one I met tonight is anyone I could even vaguely consider spending the rest of my life with."

"No one?" Joe refused to analyze the spurt of relief he felt.

"No one," she repeated gloomily. "That poor guy I talked to over at the refreshment table spent the better part of an hour telling me all about his wife who divorced him last year, and he can't understand why. I could have given him a couple of hints, but I didn't have either the nerve or the heart. All the rest of the men seemed to be attached to someone."

"Remember that the reason for this party was to introduce Warren to eligible women. If that were your goal, would you invite other single men?"

Addy frowned. "Probably not. Warren would be bound

to suffer in comparison.'' She began to feel a little better. ''In fact, I'll bet Cookie invited the worst specimens of masculinity she could find.''

Joe grinned at her. ''Thank you.''

''You know what I mean. Besides, you were an afterthought.''

''Hopefully, next time I won't be a thought at all.'' Joe glanced around in annoyance. ''This is definitely not my scene.''

Nor was it Addy's, he realized, but what was? She'd fit very well into his bedroom. The sudden thought ratcheted up his blood pressure. He could picture her wearing a thin wisp of semitransparent silk. Low-cut, with a thin lace bodice over her breasts. His heart began to pound as his mind obligingly supplied an image of one pert nipple peeking through the lace. He elaborated on his fantasy. The nightgown should be narrowly cut, to show off her long, slender legs.

Damn! Why were they wasting their time being bored at this stupid party when they could be back at his place doing what he really wanted to do, making love? Slowly and thoroughly all night long.

But what did Addy want? Probably not that, he conceded. But he wouldn't know until he tried. And he had to try. His need for her was growing. Growing every time he touched her. Every time he caught her eye and she smiled at him as if the two of them shared a joke that nobody else knew.

Even if she drew the line at going to bed with him, she would probably let him kiss her. She seemed to enjoy kissing him. The thought gave him hope.

Addy misinterpreted his abstracted expression. ''Are you getting a headache?''

''Yes.'' Joe grabbed at the excuse. ''Let's get out of here.''

''I'm game. How do we escape?''

"We find our hostess, lie through our teeth about what a wonderful time we had and run for the door."

Addy took his arm, relishing the feel of his hard muscles through the smooth material of his suit jacket, and they went in search of Cookie.

Cookie was clearly loath to let Joe leave, and she made such a determined effort to extract an invitation from him to his home that Addy was embarrassed for her. Finally, when it became clear even to Cookie that no invitation would be forthcoming, she allowed them to leave, with the promise or threat—Addy wasn't sure which—of inviting them over for a cozy little dinner one night soon.

Twenty minutes later Joe pulled up in front of his garage and parked the car. He cut the engine as he searched for an approach to use to get her first into his arms and then into his bed.

"Thanks for taking me to the party," Addy said.

"It's part of our deal," he said absently.

For some reason his reminder of why he'd taken her annoyed her immensely. Scrambling out of the car, she started toward the cottage.

"Hey." Joe hurried after her, seeing his tentative plans for the evening dissolving and not understanding why. "Where are you going?"

"Home," she said, trying not to let her irritation show. She wasn't even sure why she was irritated. After all, she knew why Joe was going out with her. So why should it bother her that he'd reminded her?

"I'll walk you over," Joe said.

Was he walking her home because of his innate good manners or because he was going to kiss her good-night? Addy felt a jolt of excitement, which was immediately drowned out by uncertainty. How did good-night kisses work? Was she supposed to invite him inside and let him kiss her there? Or was she supposed to say good-night on her doorstep and let him kiss her there? Nervously she chewed on her lower lip. What if she said good-night and then waited for him to kiss her and he didn't? He'd realize that was what she wanted and he'd feel sorry for her. Her skin crawled. She didn't want Joe to feel sorry for her. She wasn't exactly sure what she wanted from him, but pity definitely wasn't it.

Her footsteps slowed as they approached the cottage.

Joe frowned at her. "What's the matter?"

"Nothing," Addy muttered. The problem was that she wanted him to kiss her again, she admitted. It mattered to her. Mattered far more than it should. But that was an area that she didn't want to explore. Instinctively, she knew that she wasn't going to like the answer.

"How much did you have to drink?" Joe followed his own line of thought, based on his experiences with his mother.

"Three glasses of a great peach-flavored iced tea," she said. "I rarely drink, and never to excess."

"Are you morally opposed to alcohol?" he asked curiously.

"No, only to making a fool of myself. I found out in college that one beer and my mouth tends to operate independently of my mind."

She slowly climbed up the two steps to her front door. Should she invite him in or say good-night at the door? She dithered.

"What is the matter with you?" Joe asked worriedly. "Did that fool Warren scare you that much?"

"No, I'm just trying to decide what I should do with you," Addy blurted out.

Joe shot her a curiously intent glance. "What are my choices?"

"I meant, what is a woman supposed to do when a man brings her home from a date?" She skirted what was really bothering her. "Do I offer you my hand or invite you in?"

"Invite me in for a glass of water," he said.

"Water? I thought it was coffee you invited a man in for after a date."

"I don't want coffee, I want water," he said reasonably.

"Then I'll give you some." Addy unlocked her door and gestured him inside. She walked into the tiny kitchen, poured him a glass of water and handed it to him. "But that still doesn't answer my question. How does a man view an invitation to come inside? For that matter, how does a man decide if he's going to kiss a woman good-night?" she finally blurted out.

Joe took a long swallow of the cold water and then sank down on the hard sofa. He yanked his tie loose, kicked off his shoes and propped his large feet up on the coffee table.

A tender smile tugged at Addy's mouth. The poor man looked exhausted. Definitely not a threat to her virtue—worse luck.

"In this day and age, a man will almost always kiss a woman good-night. It's expected."

Addy blinked. "You mean the man expects to get a good-night kiss in exchange for the date."

Joe shook his head. "No, I mean that if a man doesn't at least try to kiss a woman she's liable to think that he doesn't find her attractive. Or question his sexual orientation."

"Oh." Addy thought about that for a moment. "I'm not sure I like the sound of that. I could wind up kissing all kinds of disgusting men."

Joe chuckled. "What's the old saying? That you have to kiss a lot of frogs to find your prince?"

Discouraged, Addy sank down on the sofa beside him. "Suppose I don't want to kiss someone? Would a man take it as a put-down?"

"Depends. If you were to start rubbing your forehead about halfway though the evening and, when your date asks what's wrong, tell him that you have the most frightful headache and give him a brave little smile..."

"Like this?" Addy gave him a tentative smile.

Joe cocked his head to one side and studied her for a

long moment. "No," he finally said. "You don't look pained. You look wistful."

"Really?" Addy studied the gleam in his eye with growing excitement. "What kind of a reaction does wistful get from a man?"

Joe set his glass down on the end table and leaned closer to her. He gently brushed his lips across hers in a featherlight caress that left her feeling more frustrated than anything else. It was like throwing a thirsty man a few drops of water while leaving the water pitcher in front of him. In fact, that kiss was far more likely to raise feelings of wistfulness than to alleviate them.

She peered up at Joe and murmured, "What kind of reaction does a man kissing a wistful woman expect?"

Joe squinted off into the distance as if considering. "I suppose it would depend on why she was wistful. Although as a general rule, a man likes an enthusiastic response to his kisses. It's very off-putting to kiss a woman and have her withdraw like you just did. It makes a man question whether he's any good at it."

"I didn't withdraw when you kissed me!" Addy forgot her shyness in her need to make him understand that she didn't find his kisses unattractive.

Joe studied her for a long minute.

"But you didn't respond," he finally said.

Addy squirmed, uncomfortable with this discussion, but determined to see it through. If she was ever to find out how the male mind operated, this was her best bet, and she was determined not to lose the chance simply because she was inhibited when it came to talking about sex.

"I didn't really have much time," she defended herself. "I mean, you kissed me so fast."

"Did you like it?" Joe cut to what to him was the heart of the matter. He was almost certain from the way she'd responded earlier that she liked kissing him. If he could just get her to admit it to herself, then maybe she would be willing to consider what else they could do that she would also enjoy.

"I'm a perfectly normal woman, and you're an attractive man," she hedged. "What's not to like?"

"Does that mean that you want to kiss every attractive man that you meet?" he persisted.

"No, it doesn't! And we seem to have wandered rather far from the point. In fact, at the moment I can't remember what it was."

Joe grinned at her. "The effect of my kisses?"

"More likely the effect of all your analysis."

"You're right. What's needed is action, not talk." He lost patience with the intellectual approach and decided to try a more physical one. The worst thing that could happen would be that she'd say no.

To Addy's surprise, Joe suddenly reached for her and pulled her toward him.

Addy fell forward, landing against his hard chest. She could feel the sharp edge of his belt buckle digging into her rib cage and her face was half buried against his shirt. She took a deep, steadying breath and the enticing odor of his cologne mingled with the warm masculine scent of his skin flooded her senses.

Addy wiggled into a more comfortable position and consciously tried to relax her muscles, but it was a hopeless task. There wasn't a single thing about her that was relaxed. Not her body and certainly not her mind. She was a quivering mass of need fueled by anticipation. Anticipation that Joe was going to kiss her again.

He might be doing it to demonstrate a point, but even so he wasn't immune to her closeness. She shifted slightly, allowing her hips to push up against his growing hardness. The heat of him seemed to burn through the thin silk of her dress, and she swallowed as a confusing mixture of longing and fear spiraled through her. She wanted to feel that heat inside her. She wanted to know what it felt like to share the ultimate intimacy with Joe. To be a part of him, at least for a moment.

"Generally I kiss a woman's lips. At least before I move on to other parts." Joe addressed the top of her head, which was all that was visible. He determinedly reined in his desire to pounce and devour her in a series of greedy kisses. Go slowly, he cautioned himself. Don't scare her off.

Other parts? Addy ran her tongue over her dry lips as all kinds of intoxicating images poured through her mind.

"But in order to kiss a woman's lips, I have to get to them."

Taking a deep breath, Addy lifted her head and looked up at him. "What other parts?" To her horror, what she was thinking just popped out. She could feel a fiery blush stain her cheeks.

Joe's lips lifted in a wicked grin, and he slowly traced over the rising tide of color on her flushed cheeks with the tip of his finger. A shivering sensation skated over her skin, tightening her nerve endings. "Stick with me, kid, and I'll show you the ropes," he drawled in a terrible imitation of James Cagney.

Stick with him and wind up with a broken heart. The appalling thought suddenly surfaced. No, she refused to allow her fears to take root. Joe could only break her heart if she were in love with him, and she wasn't. She just liked him. Liked him a lot. As well as respected him as a person. Sharing a few kisses couldn't possibly hurt her. Nothing that felt this good could be bad.

Joe traced his fingertip over her ear, and Addy shuddered at the sensation that shivered through her. She peered up at him, mentally urging him to shut up and kiss her before she dissolved into a puddle of smoldering need. To her relief, he finally lowered his head and unerringly found her mouth. His lips were warm and supple as they moved over hers, nibbling on her throbbing flesh. She clutched his shoulders, digging her fingers into his powerful muscles and pressing herself closer to him. The very faint shadow of his emerging beard rasped against her face, emphasizing the basic difference between them.

A tight band of need coiled around her chest, interfering with her breathing as Joe caught her lower lip between his teeth and lightly rubbed the tip of his tongue over it. A heavy flush burned itself across her cheeks, seeping into her mind and making it hard to think.

Addy twisted in his grasp, trying to push her tingling breasts closer to him. She felt confused and vaguely disoriented, but she didn't really care. All that mattered at the moment was that she continue to feel the sensations he was awakening. She had the strange feeling that there was some kind of time limit on what they were doing, and she needed to hurry, to cram in as much as she could before it expired.

Joe's tongue pushed between her lips, and Addy immediately opened her mouth, welcoming the invasion. His tongue was hot and ever-so-slightly rough as it moved against her own in an imitation of a greater intimacy. Addy's heart was beating so hard against her rib cage that she felt light-headed, as if she were weightless and the only thing holding her tethered to earth was the strength of Joe's arms wrapped around her.

Joe's lips moved, wandering slowly across her cheek, and Addy trembled as her skin tightened almost painfully.

"You have the most incredible skin," Joe muttered against her neck. "Like the softest velvet, only warm. And you smell so fantastic. Like springtime. All mixed up with quintessential woman." His words echoed meaninglessly in her ears as she arched her head back to allow his wandering lips greater access. It seemed unbelievable that just the touch of his mouth on her skin could feel so fantastic.

She wanted... Addy froze as she felt the hard warmth of his fingers slip beneath the thin strap of her dress. Her breath caught in her throat as he slowly pushed the soft material down over her arm to expose her throbbing breasts. Would he be disappointed by her shape? The worry momentarily dimmed the pleasure that had filled her.

Suppose… She gasped as his arms tightened and he lifted her toward him. His warm breath was a brand across her sensitive skin.

"You're so beautiful." Joe's muttered words echoed strangely in her ears.

Addy gulped convulsively as he licked the tip of her breast with his tongue and a fiery shard of sensation lanced through her.

"I…we…" she muttered, having absolutely no idea what she wanted to say. The only thing she was certain of was what she was feeling.

To her intense disappointment, Joe took her confused mumbles as a desire to stop. He gently pulled her dress back up and then drew her closer to his chest, holding her in what he probably thought was a comforting embrace. It wasn't. The pressure of his hard chest against her throbbing breasts was an exquisite torture that demanded relief. But it was a relief that she lacked the self-confidence to ask for.

Maybe Joe didn't want to continue making love to her. The appalling thought suddenly occurred to her. Maybe all he'd ever meant to do was to kiss her. Or maybe he'd stopped because he'd been disappointed in how she looked or reacted.

Addy felt like screaming from a potent combination of frustration, fear and uncertainty, but she beat the impulse down. Instead, she tried to extract every little bit of pleasure that she could from what contact with Joe she did have.

Seven

Addy put her papers on her coffee table and stood up, stretching to relieve her cramped muscles. She glanced back at the kitchen clock, surprised at how long it had taken her to finish planning exactly what kind of classes she was going to offer at her children's clinics.

What would Joe be doing at two o'clock on a Saturday afternoon? Her thoughts strayed to him, as they seemed to do with increasing frequency.

Uncertainly, Addy nibbled on her lower lip. Her growing preoccupation with him was beginning to make her nervous. But maybe her fascination was a natural evolution, given their strange relationship? After all, she was using him to practice her male-female relating skills. And she found their practice sessions exhilarating. A quiver trembled through her as she remembered the feel of his mouth against her tingling breasts. "Exhilarating" didn't begin to describe how he made her feel. But, hopefully, her fascination with Joe would fade to warm friendship when she started dating someone else.

At the thought of dating someone else, her gaze swung to her phone. When she'd returned from the grocery store this morning, she'd found a message from Warren White on her answering machine, telling her that he wanted to take her out to dinner tonight and for her to call him back. The message unnerved her. She didn't like Warren. She didn't like his self-centered outlook, but most especially she didn't like the way he'd made her feel when he'd tried to kiss her.

Addy shoved her fingers through her hair in frustration. It didn't make any sense. When Joe had kissed her, her reaction had been to want more. Much more. She'd wanted to ride the euphoria of his kisses to bigger and better things. Joe's kisses made her feel feminine and powerful in a way she never had before. Why was there such a drastic difference between the two men's kisses? It wasn't as if she was in love with Joe.

She didn't know anywhere near enough about him to be in love with him, she assured herself. She didn't even know what he did with his Saturday afternoons. Her father had played golf or puttered in his garden, but she'd seen no evidence that Joe played any kind of games and he employed a very competent landscaping firm to take care of his yard.

Surreptitiously pulling aside the living-room curtain, she peered out the front window toward Joe's house. There was no sign of life to be seen. Addy sighed in disappointment even though it vaguely worried her that she wanted to see him so badly. She was fast coming to the conclusion that kissing Joe was like fooling around with drugs. You quickly reached the point where your mind kept swinging between memories of your last fix and scheming about how to get the next one.

How did Joe feel about their kisses? Did he find them as mind-boggling as she did? Probably not, she conceded honestly. In fact, undoubtedly not. He was a man who was used to carrying his relationships a whole lot further than merely kissing. He probably thought what they were exchanging was rather juvenile.

And what would he consider adult? She shivered as she remembered his comment about kissing a woman's lips before moving on to other parts.

The sudden ringing of her phone interrupted her daydreams and Addy automatically started to answer it, only to pause when she realized that it could well be Warren calling back. She didn't want to talk to him before she'd had time to come up with an absolutely ironclad excuse not to go out with him.

But what if it was Joe? Her hand hovered near the phone. She'd let the answering machine take the call. If it was Joe, she'd cut in, and if it was Warren she wouldn't, she decided as it rang again.

Addy sent up a silent prayer: Please let it be Joe. Fate ignored her plea. It was Warren's slightly peevish voice she heard. Clearly he was annoyed at getting her machine again.

Addy tensed as he said that he'd stop by to see her in person when he returned from his golf game at the country club. Indecisively, Addy stared at her front door. She could stay and confront Warren like the mature woman she was, or she could leave and postpone dealing with the problem.

Leave, Addy decided as she grabbed her purse. She'd stop by Joe's house and see if he was there. If he was, she'd tell him about her plans for the clinic and ask him what he thought about them. He might not know anything about nursing, but he had a very practical turn of mind. He might see something she'd failed to take into consideration.

If he wasn't home, she would go over to the plant and see if he was there. If he wasn't, she could always see if maintenance had gotten around to painting her meeting room yet.

Addy didn't get an answer when she rang the bell of

Joe's house and a surreptitious peek in the front window revealed no sign of life. The plant then, she decided, heading for her car.

A feeling of anticipation curled through her as she pulled into the plant's almost-empty parking lot and saw Joe's black Mercedes. He was here!

Hastily parking the car, she hurried up the front walk, eager to see him. To share her plans with him.

The reception area was deserted except for a security guard who was sitting at the desk reading a magazine. He glanced up as she came in, said, "Mr. Barrington is in his office, Miss Edson," and went back to his reading.

Addy hurried down the empty hallway and stuck her head around the half-open door of Joe's office. Her heartbeat skyrocketed as she caught sight of his dark head bent over whatever it was that he was reading with such intentness.

"Busy?" she asked.

Joe glanced up, and he gave her a warm smile.

Lured by his obvious welcome, Addy walked over to his desk. "You're in a good mood for someone who's working on a Saturday."

"That's not the proper way to greet a man you're supposedly dating when you haven't seen him since—"

"Last night," Addy said dryly, intrigued by the gleaming sparks of devilment glowing in his eyes. Something deep within her responded wholeheartedly to his mood, making her feel reckless.

"Let me try again." Theatrically, she flung her shoulders back, which pushed her breasts against her Snoopy T-shirt, and made her right hip jut out. Then she murmured in the most throbbing tones she could manage, "Hello, there, big boy. I'm desolate for the sight of you. It's been hours since I've seen you."

Joe chuckled. "Forget Mae West. You aren't the type."

Addy ignored her feeling of pique at his unflattering assessment of her allure and instead concentrated on showing him she could be just as sexy as the next woman. Slinking behind his desk, she tipped his swivel chair back and peered down into his suddenly still face. Leaning closer, she allowed her hair to brush across his cheek and then slowly, deliberately, ran the tip of her tongue over her bottom lip in an action copied from a TV commercial. Encouraged by the way he was staring at her mouth, Addy started to move around him, allowing her breast to brush up against his shoulder.

It was almost her undoing. The blaze of reaction that shot through her shattered her thoughts into a million fragments that reformed into a pulsating ball of need to get closer to him. Addy froze, concentrating on hanging on to her self-control. Her effort wasn't helped any when Joe suddenly grabbed hold of her arm and pulled her toward him.

Addy landed awkwardly in his lap. For a moment, she simply relished being close to him, and then she indulged her craving to touch him by snuggling closer. Nestling her head against his shoulder, she ran her finger over his jawline. His skin felt like rasped silk scraping across the sensitive pads of her fingertips. Tiny pinpricks of excitement seeped into her flesh, racing along her nerves and heightening her awareness of him. Addy shifted slightly, the better to feel his hardening desire. Dreamily, she flexed her fingers, pressing them against his skin in an attempt to intensify the sensations building in her.

"How good you feel, handsome," Addy purred, throwing herself into the role of seductress with abandon.

Slipping her hand inside his suit jacket, she rubbed her hand over the crisp cotton shirt that covered his chest. She could feel the hard thudding of his heart against the palm of her hand. A beat that was echoed in her own body. Feeling greatly daring, she licked his skin above his collar. "And you taste even better."

A sense of satisfaction surged through her as Joe's heartbeat went into overdrive. Addy tipped her head back and peered up at him. All the humor had disappeared from his face and his features were set in rigid lines as if he were under a great deal of strain.

Deciding she might as well be hanged for a sheep as a lamb, Addy fumbled with his shirt buttons, faltering momentarily at the strength of the pleasure that surged through her as her palm scraped over the tangle of thick hair on his chest. She shoved her fingers through it, savoring the unfamiliarity of his body.

As if her action had pushed him past some limit, Joe's arms suddenly tightened around her, and he captured her mouth with a blatant hunger that fueled Addy's own excitement.

Instinctively, Addy opened her mouth, the better to accommodate his thrusting tongue. She felt as if her insides were softening, flowing toward him. Wonderingly, she rubbed her hand back and forth across his chest as she opened her mouth wider still, wanting more. Wanting so very much more.

Joe obviously shared that decision because he pushed her T-shirt up and fumbling with the clasp on her bra, finally freed it and yanked her up against him.

Addy's breath caught in her throat as her sensitive nipples scraped across his chest. Mindlessly, she wrapped her arms around his neck and allowed the sensations he was creating to wash through her. A heavy, urgent throbbing sparked to life deep within her.

"Oh, I'm so sorry! I didn't realize..." The shocked voice sliced through Addy's pleasure like a sharp knife. Embarrassment slithered over her, effectively dousing her desire. Keeping her face pressed against Joe's chest, she surreptitiously worked her T-shirt down over her bare chest.

What was happening to her? Addy wondered in confusion. How could she have changed so much that she had been willing—no not willing, eager—to kiss Joe in a place where it was quite possible that they would be interrupted?

"I didn't mean to interrupt," the young woman in her

early twenties continued, "but Mr. Blandings said that I was to bring this to you right away, sir, and..."

"Is it signed?" Joe demanded.

Addy watched with intense disappointment as the sexual tension bled out of his face, to be replaced by tension of another kind. But what kind?

With a jerky movement, Addy rebuttoned his shirt and got to her feet trying to appear nonchalant.

"Yes." The woman studiously avoided looking at Addy as she handed Joe a manila envelope. "He and his lawyer signed it, and Mr. Blandings had me bring it right over. Mr. Blandings said to tell you that the contract is absolutely ironclad. That there's no way it can be broken."

A shiver chased down Addy's spine at the expression on Joe's face. He looked like the Lord High Executioner about to spring the gallows' door. She couldn't see any trace of the teasing, indulgent man she'd been playing lighthearted sexual games with only moments before.

Apparently the young woman didn't think Joe looked any too approachable either, because she shifted nervously from one foot to the other, then finally said, "Was there anything else you wanted, sir?"

"No." Joe's smile held nothing of humor in it. "This will do it. Tell Blandings to let me know if there are any new developments."

"Certainly, sir. Ma'am." The young woman nodded vaguely in Addy's direction and beat a hasty retreat.

Addy watched her disappear and then quickly refastened her bra before she looked at Joe. He was staring down at the envelope with an expression that could only be called gloating.

"What is that?" she asked.

Joe looked up, his eyes blank, as if he'd totally forgotten she was there. "Retribution," he muttered.

David Edwards. Addy immediately made the connection.

"Edwards finally signed the papers," Joe said, confirming her conclusion. "He's been dithering all week long, trying to find some other way to raise the money, but he couldn't. So he signed. Now it's just a matter of time.''

"Joe, what are you going to do with the Edwards Corporation when you do finally get your hands on it?''

Joe frowned at her. ''Do with it? What do you mean, do with it?''

"You're a businessman. One doesn't spend the kind of money I suspect you're talking about and not know what you're getting for it.''

"I don't want to do a damn thing with Edwards's company. I just...''

"Don't want David to have it," Addy finished for him.

"I don't want any Edwards to have it! Taking away that plant is how I'm finally going to make them pay for what they did to my mother and me.''

Addy looked around his luxurious office. "Yeah, I can see what they did to you," she said wryly.

"You don't see anything!" Joe shot back. "They turned my mother into a drunk.''

Addy studied him in frustration. Why was it so hard for Joe to acknowledge his mother's role in the disastrous affair? He wasn't a stupid man. Nor was he a cruel one.

"Think, Joe! Open your eyes to everything that happened, not just the parts you want to remember.''

Joe glared at her. "I'm not so blind that I can't see that you're far more interested in Edwards than you should be.''

Addy's sense of frustration increased. How could she make Joe understand that it wasn't David Edwards she was worried about? It was him. This thirst for revenge he was harboring was not healthy. It kept him focused in the past, and the past was dead.

"If you hang around long enough, maybe you can help Edwards pick up the pieces of his empire," Joe snapped.

Addy clamped her lips together to repress a hasty retort and headed toward the door. There was no reasoning with Joe in this mood. It was futile even to try. She'd only get angry and wind up saying something to make him even madder.

"Go on, go! But I won't change my mind!" Joe yelled after her.

The way Joe was acting, she half expected him to tell her he was going to take his ball and go home, Addy thought as she hurried out of the offices, nodding absently at the security guard, who was staring at her with his mouth hanging open.

Addy pulled her car out of the parking lot and was about to head home when she suddenly remembered Warren. Trying to deal with his self-centered egotism after Joe's pigheadedness was too much even to contemplate. She'd visit Kathy, she finally decided. And she'd ignore Joe until he came to his senses.

But Addy found ignoring Joe much harder than she'd expected. Saturday evening seemed endless as she spent the time alternating between pretending to read a book and watching the lighted windows of Joe's house in the hope of catching sight of him. She didn't, and she finally gave up and went to bed at ten-thirty, worn out by her emotional turmoil.

The following morning she drove slowly past Joe's silent house as she left for church but was unable to catch even a glimpse of him. If he was home, he was keeping a very low profile.

She deliberately dawdled after mass, joining in the coffee-and-donut session in the church basement in an attempt to try to fill a little time. Finally, after four cups of coffee and almost an hour's worth of meaningless conversation with people that she wasn't all that keen to talk to anyway, she got in her car and headed home.

She wanted to see Joe. She finally faced the fact. More than wanted, on some level that she didn't clearly understand, she needed to see him. It didn't matter that he was mad at her or that as far as she was concerned he was

behaving irrationally, she still had to see him. And maybe
she should, she told herself, rationalizing her desire. After
all, she couldn't very well get him to change his mind if
she wasn't there to keep pushing him. Without her to inject
a note of sanity, he'd simply wallow in his thoughts of
revenge. She nodded decisively as she parked the car in
front of the cottage. It was her moral duty to see him.

Hurriedly changing into jeans and a hunter-green T-shirt,
Addy headed toward his house. She went by way of the
garage, so that she could check to make sure he hadn't left
while she had been at church. He hadn't. His car was still
there. Satisfied, she hurried toward the front door and
pressed down on the doorbell. Nothing happened. She
counted to twenty and then pressed again.

Why wasn't he answering? she wondered. She knew he
was there. He never walked anywhere. Was he not answering because he didn't want to talk to her? The thought
depressed her momentarily, but she refused to let it dis-
courage her. Letting their argument drag out would be
bound to make it worse. She pushed the doorbell down for
a third time and then jumped when the door suddenly
opened in midchime to reveal Joe. But a Joe who looked
very different than he had the last time she'd seen him. His
thick, dark hair was disheveled, his eyes were bloodshot
and his face was pale with hectic blotches of color high on
both cheeks. He looked awful.

"Stop that dammed racket!" he bit out.

"What's wrong?" She ignored his ill humor.

"And you're supposed to be a nurse," he muttered.
"What do you think is the matter with me? I'm sick." He
turned and stomped toward the living room.

Worried, Addy followed him.

Joe flung himself onto the couch and closed his eyes.

Addy gently pushed his damp hair back from his forehead, wincing at how hot he felt. "Have you seen a doctor?"

He peered blearily up at her. "A doctor? On a Sunday? You've got to be kidding."

"You need to see a doctor," she insisted. "You're burning up with fever."

"I don't need a doctor to tell me I've got the flu. Half the office was out with it last week."

"But—"

"Don't nag! My head hurts," he added plaintively, and Addy wanted nothing so much as to take him in her arms and comfort him. He looked so miserable.

"When was the last time you had aspirin?" she asked.

Joe blinked uncertainly. "Aspirin?"

"Aspirin and fluids are the traditional remedy for flu."

"Don't have any aspirin," he muttered. "I don't get headaches."

"No, you just give them," she said dryly. "What about liquids? Have you taken any?"

"I tried to drink some orange juice last night, but it tasted strange."

Honestly, Addy thought in exasperation, the man was hopeless. She started toward the door.

"Don't go," Joe muttered, and Addy looked back at him in surprise. Somehow, she wouldn't have ever expected Joe to ask anyone to do anything for him.

"I'll be right back," she said soothingly. "I'm just going over to the cottage. Unlike you, I do have aspirin."

"Hurry up," he ordered.

Addy returned within minutes to find Joe still lying on the couch staring at the door.

"What took you so long?" he grumbled.

"Irritability is one of the first signs of flu."

"I am not irritable!"

Addy's lips twitched, but she held her peace. She poured a little water from the bottle she'd brought back with her into a glass and handed it to him along with two aspirin.

Joe's hand shook, and he spilled the water down the front of his blue T-shirt.

"Damn!" He sank back down on the sofa and closed his eyes.

Addy took the now-empty glass from his limp fingers. "You need to take the aspirin." She refilled the glass.

Joe opened his fever-bright eyes and glared at her. "I'm dying, and you're blathering about aspirin?"

"Yup," Addy said. Slipping her arm under his shoulders, she levered him up, supporting his head against her chest. She could feel the prickly ends of his hair pressing against her bare arm.

Addy swallowed uneasily, unnerved by her awareness of him as a sexual being under the present circumstances. She shouldn't be thinking this way, she tried to tell herself. Joe was sick. She should be thinking of him as a patient. She'd never had any trouble maintaining an emotional distance from an adult patient before. So why couldn't she now?

"Put the aspirin in your mouth," she ordered, deliberately trying to regain something of her professional manner.

Joe obediently put them in his mouth and then gulped down the water from the glass she held to his lips.

He closed his eyes and collapsed back against the sofa as if the slight effort had exhausted him.

"Don't go back to sleep until I get your shirt off."

Joe opened one eye and turned his unfocused gaze toward her. "Come again?"

"It's wet." Addy gestured to the damp shirt. "You need to take it off." She deftly grabbed the hem and yanked it up over his head, trying to ignore the enticing view of his bare chest. "Wait here while I get you a clean shirt and a blanket. The air-conditioning in here is chilly."

"A blanket! I feel like I'm burning up, and you want to get me a blanket?"

Addy ignored his mutters and sprinted upstairs, looking for his bedroom. The first two rooms she looked into were obviously guest bedrooms that didn't appear to have been touched since the decorator had finished.

She whistled in surprise as she opened the double doors

at the end of the hall and found the master bedroom. An exquisite green, gold and ivory tapestry carpet covered the floor of the huge room, but the dominating feature was the antique tester bed. Obviously hand-carved out of what looked to be mahogany, it had a white hand-knit canopy. It was the embodiment of every adolescent fantasy she'd ever had. She wanted to bounce on the bed and stretch out on it. With Joe. She wanted to share that bed with Joe.

But what did Joe want? Certainly not to get involved with her on any meaningful level. And making love with him would certainly be meaningful. At least, it would be to her. What it might mean to Joe she had no idea. Not only was the average male mind a closed book to her, but Joe was in no sense of the word average.

And complicating her ability to understand him was his sterile upbringing. He didn't view relationships as supportive. He saw them as binding. As a way to get someone to go against their own best interests. The most she could hope for with Joe was that he'd indulge in an affair with her. And if he'd wanted to do that, surely he would have continued kissing her the night of the party.

The sound of Joe's plaintive voice calling her drifted up the stairs, and she hurriedly opened drawers until she found one with underwear in it. Grabbing a shirt, she was about to close the drawer when she caught sight of something glittery. Curious, she picked it up.

It was a small, thin package. She turned it over and frowned when she realized what it was. What did Joe need a condom for? she thought and then winced at the stupidity of the question. He was a grown man with a grown man's appetites. She should be happy he was adult enough to make sure there were no unexpected repercussions to his lovemaking. She rubbed her thumb over the slick, foil package. But even if that was the way she was supposed to feel, she didn't. She didn't want Joe making love to someone else. The very thought sent a corrosive surge of frustration and anger spiraling through her.

She shoved the package into her pocket and thoughtfully headed back downstairs.

Joe spent most of the day drifting in and out of a restless sleep, but to her relief his fever finally broke that evening.

"You'll live," Addy announced as she shook down the thermometer.

Joe shifted uncomfortably. "I don't feel like it," he grumbled. "I feel sticky and…"

"Don't forget grumpy." She handed him another glass of water. "Drink that."

"I'm not thirsty." He stuck out his lower lip.

Addy swallowed a smile. He looked adorable. Like a small boy determined to be obstructive. She wanted to lean over and kiss his thrusting lip.

"I want a shower." His announcement took her by surprise.

"Tomorrow," she countered. "You may have shed the fever, but you're still showing the effects of it. You're weak and dizzy."

And horny as hell, Joe thought grimly. His body might be weak, but his mind knew exactly what it wanted. It wanted to get Addy into bed. It wanted to strip her clothes off and caress her fantastic body. It wanted to kiss her breasts and take the nipples into his mouth and taste them. It wanted to learn every nuance of every soft curve she had.

The very thought sent a surge of adrenaline through him strong enough to bring him to his feet. He staggered slightly and grabbed the end of the sofa to steady his rubbery legs.

"Will you listen to reason? You can't even stand on your own two feet."

"Maybe I need a little help," he said slowly as an idea of how to get her into his bedroom suddenly occurred to him. Now, if he could just figure out how to get her out of her clothes. He lurched from the sofa to the end table, deliberately exaggerating his dizziness.

Addy shook her head and gave up trying to talk him out

of it. He never listened to good advice when he was well; he was hardly likely to start when he was feeling out of sorts. The best thing for her to do would be to go along with him and make sure he didn't fall and fracture something.

"Come on. I'll help." She slipped her arms around his waist and supported him as he staggered up to his bedroom. Once there, he shoved open one of the doors in the bedroom's far wall, and Addy found herself in the most incredible bathroom she'd ever seen. It was a huge room full of gleaming copper, gold-flecked marble tile and mirrors. Lots of mirrors.

As well as a tub, she realized when she saw the oversized whirlpool tub sitting in lonely splendor against the far wall.

"You can take a bath," Addy said, thinking that he'd be less likely to fall if he were sitting. "It's just the thing for soothing all the aches the flu left," she added when he frowned and looked toward the shower.

"You sit here." She deposited him on the toilet seat and hurriedly began to run the water. To her relief, Joe didn't say anything. He simply sat there, as if the effort of getting upstairs had taken more out of him than he'd expected. Or was willing to admit. Poor dear, she thought. He obviously was not sick very often, because he had no experience at handling it.

When she had the tub half-filled with warm water, she switched on the whirlpool jets and turned to Joe. He was sitting hunched over, with his elbows on his knees, staring down at the floor. Doubtfully, her gaze swung back to the tub. If he were to fall getting in and hit his head... A feeling of panic swamped her. He could drown.

She'd have to help him. After all, she was a nurse. She'd seen thousands of naked men in her time. Nudity of and by itself wasn't particularly sexy, she reassured herself.

"Come on," she said brightly. "I'll help you into the tub, and then I'll wait for you in the bedroom while you soak."

"Yes, nanny." Joe staggered to his feet, his mind busily considering possibilities. Her waiting in his bedroom was better than having her go back downstairs, but not much.

"The shirt first," she said.

"The shirt," Joe repeated. He yanked it over his head, wavering slightly as the movement upset his balance.

Addy grabbed for him, clutching him around his waist. She could feel his bare chest against her cheek and the springy texture of his body hair disconcerted her.

"Careful," she muttered, not even sure in her own mind whether she was talking to him or herself. All she knew for certain was that she found Joe's body fascinating. And it was a fascination that was growing with added exposure, not dissipating.

"S'okay," he muttered and, unzipping his jeans, kicked them and his shorts off.

Addy was very careful to keep her gaze firmly fixed on a spot over his left shoulder, despite the almost overwhelming impulse to glance down the length of his magnificent body.

Joe glanced up at her carefully still face and felt a surge of excitement at her expression. Despite her background in nursing, she wasn't the least bit blasé about his nudity. Now if he could just figure out... He stiffened as an idea occurred to him. It just might work.

"Get into the tub," she ordered. "You may be used to standing around naked having conversations, but I'm not."

"You aren't naked," Joe pointed out, but to her relief he obligingly took her arm and staggered toward the tub. Keeping his grip on her as if fearful of falling, he climbed in. Carefully timing it, he suddenly plopped down, pulling her in with him. Addy landed across his body with a splash that sent water everywhere.

Addy yelped in shock as her body was assaulted by sensation on all levels. The warm, bubbling water soaked her clothes, making her skin more sensitive to other stimuli. Such as the feel of his hard chest against her shoulder and of his muscled thighs against her soft hips. Addy swallowed nervously as she felt his aroused masculinity pressing against her.

She took a deep breath, trying to think, but it was hard. Her mind was so overwhelmed with sensation that there wasn't much room left over for rational thought.

Uncertainly, she peered up into Joe's face. His eyes were closed but he didn't look peaceful. He looked...tense, she finally decided. Tense because she was lying in his lap? Could he have deliberately pulled her into his bath? She found the idea exhilarating, but not very plausible. She didn't have the kind of body that drove men to those lengths. The whole thing was probably no more than an accident caused by his weakness.

"Why did you do that?" Addy finally asked.

"I was so overcome with lust that I pulled you into the tub to have my way with you." Joe told her the absolute truth, knowing she'd never believe it.

"How?"

Joe opened one eye and peered at her. "Well, nature equipped men and women differently. Men have a—"

"I know that! What I meant was, how would you go about making love to someone in a bathtub?"

"Very carefully."

Addy giggled nervously. "I should think so. Just imagine what would happen if you were to start breathing heavily at the wrong moment. You could wind up with your lungs full of water."

"You worry too much." Joe pulled her up toward him and covered her mouth with his. The heat from his lips was only slightly hotter than the water that bubbled around her. She felt as if she were immersed in his kiss. As if it surrounded her on all sides. She shifted slightly, trying to fit herself more closely against him, to intensify the sensation of being a part of him.

Unfortunately her movement sent a wave of water over her face and she choked.

Joe sighed. "You were right. Scratch lovemaking in the water. We'll have to do something else."

Rats! Addy mentally cursed her awkwardness.

"Soap," he announced.

"Soap?"

Joe nodded. "I'm too tired to move, and since you're already all wet you can help. But first…"

He grabbed the hem of her shirt and pulled it up over her head.

"Better," Joe declared, "but the shoes have to go."

Addy glanced down at her feet and was surprised to realize that she was still wearing shoes. She hastily pulled them off and dropped them over the side of the tub.

"Better still, but your jeans are irritating my skin."

Addy's sense of spiraling anticipation was suddenly arrested. Much as she craved feeling his blatant masculinity against her bare flesh, if she took off her jeans he'd see the silvery stretch marks on her stomach. He hadn't seemed to notice the ones on her breasts, but those on her belly were much more prominent.

Addy dithered as she felt him fumbling with the tab on her jeans. Slowly, as if expecting an objection, Joe pulled the zipper down.

She tried to stem her growing fears. It wouldn't matter; the water would hide the marks, and she'd wrap a towel around herself when they got out of the water.

A sense of inevitability rolled through her as Joe peeled the jeans down over her hips. She had the weird feeling that her whole life had been building toward this moment, and now that it had finally arrived she fully intended to savor every single second of it. She wiggled out of them, sending yet more water splashing out onto the tile floor. Finally getting them off, she picked them up to toss out when the small silver packet dropped out of a pocket.

The condom! Addy winced in embarrassed dismay as she watched the packet dancing on the bubbling surface of the water. She risked a quick glance up into Joe's face, hoping that he might not have noticed. A flush burned across her cheeks as she realized that he was watching the floating packet with a bemused expression.

"Umm...that's...it's..." Addy fumbled for something to say, for some innocuous excuse for having a condom in her pocket, but she couldn't think of a single thing.

"A condom," Joe finished her sentence for her.

"I know that!" she muttered.

"Do you always put condoms in your bathwater?" He seemed no more than mildly curious. "Is this some kind of medical advance that I haven't heard of?"

He picked it up and set it on the tub's rim.

Addy decided that since she didn't have anything to say, she'd say nothing. She'd simply ignore the whole incident.

"I was going to soap you." She looked around for a washcloth. She didn't see one. "But there aren't any washcloths."

"Improvise." He leaned his head back against the tub and closed his eyes.

Improvise? Addy studied his pale features as she considered his words. Improvise with what? Absently, she picked up the bar of white soap and began to rub it between her hands. She watched as a large soap bubble squeezed between her fingers. The overhead light broke against it, splintering into a rainbow of colors.

She felt as if she were enclosed in a soap bubble, too. Isolated from her normal, everyday world.

She peered up into Joe's face through the thick screen of her bronze lashes. His stillness seemed to underline her feelings. It was so very quiet. The only sound in the room was the faint hiss of the tub's whirlpool jets. Normal rules didn't seem to hold here. And that being so...

Addy took a deep breath and slowly began to spread the soap bubbles across her breasts. This was no time to wallow in shyness, she told herself. She might never get another chance to embellish the fantastic sensations she'd felt when she'd pressed her bare chest against his.

Mentally gathering her courage, Addy leaned forward, lightly brushing herself against his chest. His dense body hair scraped across her sensitive nipples, sending a jolt of pleasure through her. She closed her eyes, the better to concentrate on the feelings, and pressed harder. A feverish flush burned its way across her cheeks as her nipples convulsed into tight, aching buds. She felt hot. Burning hot. Hot enough to vaporize the water she was sitting in.

A heavy throbbing started to grow in her abdomen as she slowly rubbed her breasts back and forth across his chest. It made her feel disoriented, out of control of both the situation and her own reaction to it.

Addy's ragged breath whistled through her slightly parted lips, and she moved slightly, rubbing her hips over his hardness. The throbbing in her abdomen accelerated, twisting her emotions to a higher pitch.

Addy forced open her heavy eyelids and gazed up into Joe's face. He hadn't moved a muscle. It was as if he were totally unaffected by the sensations she was experiencing.

A feeling of pique shook her. He might be a lot more experienced than she was, but surely he should be feeling something? The emotion couldn't all be on her side, could it?

Her eyes focused on his slightly parted lips, and she inched forward, drawn by the irresistible thought of kissing him. As her lips met his, she finally got a reaction from Joe. His arms closed around her, and he pulled her up against him with a ferocity she found eminently satisfying. Addy shivered as he traced over her lower lip with the tip of his tongue and she opened her mouth, inviting deeper intimacy.

Quick to take advantage of her invitation, he shoved his tongue inside and began to stroke it hotly over her inner cheeks.

Addy's arms tightened around his neck as tremors of reaction began to overload her nervous system. She found that she was shaking, totally unable to control the emotions roiling through her.

Joe's arms tightened and he raised his head, staring down into her taut features as if looking for an answer to a question she hadn't heard.

"You make a great washcloth," he finally said.

Addy felt a chill feather over her wet skin. He seemed to view their lovemaking as little more than a romantic interlude of no great import. Her pride wouldn't let him see just how deeply moving she found it.

"The water is getting cold." She decided to break it off before he did.

"Do we care?" he asked, snuggling her closer to his chest.

Addy clenched her muscles to control their unfortunate tendency to tremble and said, "You've had the flu. If you get chilled, you could come down with pneumonia."

"If you say so." He dropped his arms, inexplicably leaving her feeling bereft. "Get me a towel, would you?"

Get out of the tub and walk across the room stark naked? Let him see her body's every imperfection? No way. Addy instinctively rejected the idea. Not if she had to sit here until she turned into a prune.

"Whatever happened to chivalry?" she asked.

"Hadn't you heard? It's dead. Feminism killed it. Get the towel."

"No." Addy flatly refused.

"Oh, all right." Joe gently pushed her aside and got to his feet, sending water splashing over the sides of the tub.

Addy's eyes widened as her gaze travelled up over the strong line of his thighs to his groin. She gulped as a feeling of longing burned through her. He was so gorgeous. So absolutely perfect. And so overwhelmingly different from her.

Mesmerized, she watched the smooth ripple of his muscles beneath his wet skin as he walked across the room toward the only rack that had any towels on it. He was so graceful. He moved as if to music. A symphony. But what symphony?

A dreamy smile curved her lips. Definitely one by Beethoven. Robust, firm, definite, bigger than life, building toward a climax to blow one's mind.

"Here."

Addy reluctantly surfaced from her fantasies in time to see a fluffy blue towel come flying toward her. She automatically grabbed it before it landed in the water and, holding it in front of her as a shield, hastily wrapped it around herself.

She shot Joe a nervous glance, fearful that he might have seen her imperfections, but he was leaning against the wall. His eyes were closed and his towel was loosely clutched in one hand. He looked totally exhausted.

Worried, Addy tucked the end of her oversized towel between her breasts, sarong-style, and stepped out of the tub.

Joe needed to get dry and into bed just as soon as possible. Her mouth dried as anticipation raced through her veins. By himself, she lectured herself. Joe wasn't up to making love to her.

Trying to keep her mind blank, Addy took the towel out of his limp fingers and began to rub it across the broad line of his shoulders.

"What are you doing?" Joe's voice sounded slightly blurred.

"Getting you dry." She forced a brisk note into her voice. "It's either the towel or blow on you and I doubt that would be very effective."

Joe felt the muscles in his thighs tighten at the thought of her warm breath wafting over his skin, warming it to a fever pitch. He took a deep, steadying breath, trying to control his instinctive reaction.

The scent of her perfume drifted into his nostrils, reminding him as it always did of sweet-smelling flowers and golden summer sunlight. Of a green meadow that stretched to the end of his imagination. But this time the meadow wasn't empty, he realized in some surprise. Addy was in it. He swallowed as his imaginary creation began to run through the tall, flower-tangled grass. Multicolored flower petals were stuck to her bare skin, the wind was lifting her silky hair and her bare breasts were bouncing slightly as she moved. An overpowering urge to touch her, to explore her body with his eyes and his hands and his mouth shook him.

Longingly, he peered down at her. She was so earnestly drying his belly and trying to pretend that she didn't notice how aroused he was. A feeling of tenderness filled him.

While he knew that making love to her when he was so tired was not a good idea, there was a lot of ground between actual penetration and foreplay. There was no reason he couldn't indulge his desires to that extent, he rationalized. No reason that he couldn't snuggle up beside her in his bed and savor the feel of her soft, yielding curves against him. All he had to do was to lure her into bed with him.

Addy didn't notice his calculating expression. Her entire concentration was on the feel of his muscles beneath the rough material of the towel. Of the warm, soapy scent of his skin as she rubbed it dry. Her movements became jerkier as her drying took her down his body. Down over his flat belly.

She gulped, trying to pretend that she wasn't aware of the fact that he was definitely responding to her ministrations. This is not the time, she desperately told herself.

Joe swayed slightly, his chest brushing up against her shoulder, and she hurriedly finished the job and tossed the towel on the floor.

"Come on. You need to get into bed," she ordered, hoping she didn't sound as breathless as she felt.

"Thank you," Joe muttered, and took a wavering step toward the door.

Addy hastily grabbed him and supported him as he staggered toward the bed. Once there, she tried to lever him down, but he suddenly seemed to collapse. He fell across the bed taking her with him.

Addy gulped at the feel of his heavy arm holding her pinned to the mattress. The heat from his body was burning into her skin from shoulder to thigh, making her excruciatingly aware of him in every fiber of her being.

She shouldn't stay here, she thought distractedly. She should remove herself from temptation. Tentatively she wiggled and Joe's grip tightened as if in protest even though his eyes were closed and he seemed to be totally unaware of her. Addy swallowed nervously as she felt the scalding heat of him pressed up against her bare thigh. Almost unaware of her. Maybe it wouldn't hurt if she were just to stay here for a while. Joe didn't seem to mind. In fact, he seemed determined to keep her near.

Fascinated, Addy studied the way his dark lashes stood out in stark relief against the paleness of his skin. He had such thick lashes. She wanted to touch them. To explore their texture. To see if they were as soft as his hair or as prickly as his emerging beard. The urge to find out was irresistible.

She carefully scooted closer to him and pressed her mouth against his left lash. It felt strange against her lips. Strange, but somehow very right.

"What are you doing?" Joe opened his eyes and looked intently at her.

"I was curious about what your eyelashes felt like," she said honestly.

"Eyelashes?" Joe muttered. "What do eyelashes feel like? No, never mind. I'll find out myself."

To Addy's surprise, Joe levered himself up on one elbow, hovering over her. But his nearness didn't make her feel threatened. It filled her with a wild sense of reckless excitement. Intellectually she knew full well that lying in bed with a naked man was a very bad idea, but emotionally she couldn't get beyond the fact that the naked man was

Joe, her Joe, and she wanted everything he was willing to give to her.

Joe's lips lightly brushed across her eyelids.

Addy jerked in reaction as a shivery sensation shot through her. How could such a simple caress feel so good? she wondered in confusion. How could... She lost her train of thought as his lips began to wander over her face and the feeling escalated. Her eyelids felt weighted, and they slowly closed. She could feel the warmth from his breath drifting across her skin, tightening it, and she shifted restlessly, craving more.

"Of course, one should have a control group in any experiment," Joe murmured, giving in to his compulsion to touch her breasts. He awkwardly tugged one end of her towel loose and pushed it aside.

Addy tensed, glancing worriedly down toward her stomach, but between the room's dim light and the rumpled towel she didn't think he could see her flaws. And then Joe rubbed his fingers across her soft curves and she ceased to think at all and simply felt. He cupped her breast with his hand and lightly flicked his thumb over her nipple. Sensations poured through her, interfering with her breathing.

"So beautiful." Joe's words echoed meaninglessly in her ears. "So absolutely perfect." He lowered his head and licked his tongue across the tip of her breast.

Addy gasped as the nipple convulsed into a tight, throbbing bud of desire. Clutching his head, she pulled him closer, wanting to intensify the sensation. Her fingers threaded themselves through his silky hair, holding him tightly as he took her nipple in his mouth and suckled.

Wave upon wave of reaction crashed through her, collecting deep in her abdomen where it coalesced into a burning sense of urgency. She barely noticed when Joe fumbled to open the foil packet she hadn't even realized he'd carried out of the bathroom. It didn't really seem important. The only important thing was that he not stop.

A muffled gasp escaped from between her clenched teeth

as Joe slipped his hand between her legs and lightly rubbed his finger over the slick, satiny surface. The aching need in her tightened unbearably, and she twisted in agitation. She felt as if she were about to break apart from the force of the emotions he was generating.

Time seemed suspended, her entire being poised on the brink of some momentous discovery, a discovery she was sure would irrevocably change her sense of who and what she was forever. She moaned in frustration as Joe slipped between her legs and carefully positioned himself.

She could hear him saying something, but the words echoed meaninglessly in her ears. Nothing seemed to have any substance beyond her driving need to follow this feeling through to its end.

Acting on an instinct as old as time itself, Addy wrapped her arms around his waist, pulled him down at the same time that she dug her heels into the bed and pushed upward.

Instead of the escalation of pleasure that she'd expected, jagged shards of pain ripped through her. She bit down hard on her lip to contain the anguished moan that bubbled up in her throat. She'd heard that the first time a woman made love there was some discomfort, but even so she didn't want Joe to stop. She didn't want him to stop because she loved him. The unexpected bit of self-knowledge hit her with the force of a blow, giving her a welcome sense of numbness. Somehow she had committed the monumental folly of falling in love with him.

Joe's driving need suddenly reached its apex, and he went rigid as shock waves of sensation surged through him, leaving him limp and gasping for breath. Gulping in great lungfuls of air, he slowly surfaced through the layers of pleasure that had inundated him, to became aware of his surroundings. And what he had done. His skin chilled as the full impact hit him. He'd made love to Addy!

He stared down at her in horror. How could he have done that? He hadn't meant for it to go that far. What would she think? Worse yet, what would she expect?

"I didn't mean to do that." Joe struggled to his knees, his movements clumsy and uncoordinated. His mind felt muddled from the aftermath of the flu and the most fantastic sexual encounter of his life.

Addy crushed an impulse to burst into tears and then smack him. Smack him hard enough to make him share some of the pain she was feeling. She had thought what they were sharing was so wonderful, and that was all he could say!

"I mean..." Joe closed his eyes, trying to still his whirling thoughts.

"I understand exactly what you mean." Addy cut him off. She couldn't stand much more of this. If she didn't get out of here, she was going to start to yell at him. And the way she felt at the moment, she might not be able to stop once she started.

She scrambled out of bed, barely noticing as the movement sent a wave of physical pain through her. The pain in her heart was far too great. Hastily grabbing Joe's bathrobe from the chair, she all but ran for the door. She needed time. Time alone to put what had happened in perspective.

Joe watched her go with a sinking feeling of loss. He shouldn't let her go like that, he thought. He should go after her and try to make her understand. He grimaced. The problem was that he didn't understand himself, so how could he hope to make Addy understand? He started to get up, but the room seemed to sway around him and he collapsed back on the bed. Within seconds he was deeply asleep.

Eight

Addy craned her neck to get a better view of Joe's house. It didn't help. She still couldn't see any sign of life. She glanced down at her watch. Could he still be asleep? It was almost noon. She knew he wasn't at work, because she'd called his office and been told that Mr. Barrington would not be in today.

Uncertainly, she twisted a stray curl around her forefinger as she tried to decide what to do. Her gut reaction was to stay right here in her cottage. Indefinitely. As long as she was here, she didn't have to face what had happened. Didn't have to deal with it.

Sighing, Addy leaned her head against the cool glass of the window and stared blindly at Joe's house. Tempting as the idea was, she simply couldn't do it. For one thing, she'd run out of food very shortly. For another, it wouldn't solve anything.

Restlessly, she turned away and, walking over to her sofa, plopped down on it. But could the situation be solved?

That was the sixty-four-thousand-dollar question. Despite having worried the problem around her mind for most of last night, she still couldn't think of a single way to bring about a happy ending.

How could she have committed the incredibly stupid act of falling in love with Joe Barrington? she demanded of herself. He'd never made any secret of the fact that he was not husband material. And having made love to her undoubtedly hadn't changed his mind on that score. She squirmed in embarrassment as she remembered his words of last night.

She might have found the experience the most fantastic of her life, but clearly he hadn't. While all she'd been able to think about was doing it again, Joe's first response had been to regret it.

Addy blew out her breath in a long gust. All things considered, Joe's reaction was hardly surprising. Given his background, he was hardly likely to have any good feelings about marriage and families. And was never likely to develop any as long as he wallowed in the past. He had to come to terms with the past to ever grow beyond it. But he didn't want to come to terms with it, she conceded. He wanted to get revenge.

Which left her where? Addy followed the movement of a dust mote through the stray shaft of sunshine filtering in through the window. She remembered a piece of advice in one of her psychiatry texts: distance yourself from your own problems. Pretend that a patient has brought your problem to you to solve.

Addy frowned, feeling ridiculous, but she was desperate. Somehow, she had to come up with a plan of action that would allow her to face Joe again. Face him and put their friendship back on track because if she couldn't... A feeling of panic ripped through her, but she quickly walled it off.

"Good morning." Addy addressed her imaginary patient. "Let me get this straight, Miss. You have fallen in love with a man who has clearly stated that he doesn't want any kind of a permanent relationship. He reacted to having made love to you much in the same manner as a man caught robbing a bank. Outrage, horror and embarrassment. You lost your temper, shouted at him and stormed out. You are now hiding in your house, and he is in his and you haven't got the nerve to do anything about it.''

Addy winced at her recitation of the bald facts. ''That about sums it up,'' she muttered. ''What do you recommend I do?''

''Cut your losses and get out of the relationship,'' Addy answered herself. ''The chances of getting him to change his mind about marriage, especially marriage to you, are virtually nil. You've learned a little about men from him—take what you've learned and go look for a husband elsewhere.''

Addy instinctively shook her head at her own good advice. She couldn't imagine making love to another man. The very idea made her feel faintly nauseous. She finally faced the fact that if she couldn't have Joe, she didn't want anyone. And that being the case, maybe she ought to be focusing on how to get him to fall in love with her.

Addy snorted. If that was her goal, she should be in church praying, because it was going to take a miracle to pull that off.

''God helps those who help themselves,'' she reminded herself, thinking it was a lousy way to run a world. If she could help herself, she wouldn't need divine assistance.

One thing was certain—to get Joe to fall in love with her, she had to be near him. And in order to get near, she somehow had to convince him that she wasn't trying to tie him down. That she viewed what they'd shared as little more than a pleasant experience and that she still intended to try to marry someone else. Was she that good an actress? She'd have to be, she thought grimly, because the alternative was to lose Joe.

Determinedly, Addy forced her reluctant feet to move

toward the door. The longer she waited, the harder it would be. And not only that, but the longer she waited, the more time Joe would have to construct defenses against her.

She'd use the excuse of wanting to see how he was this morning after his bout of the flu, and exactly what she said would depend on what he said, she decided, heading toward his house.

Joe grabbed the phone in his study in the middle of the first ring, hoping it was Addy. Even though he didn't have the slightest idea what to say to her, he still wanted to hear her voice. Even if it was nothing more than to hear her berate him, it was better than not hearing her at all.

"Yes?" He made an effort to moderate his voice.

"Mr. Barrington, this is Jasper Blandings. Your personal assistant gave me your home phone. I hope I'm not disturbing you?"

You don't have the power to disturb me, Joe thought as a massive feeling of disappointment settled like a lead weight in his stomach.

"Mr. Barrington? Are you too ill to talk?"

"No," Joe snapped, wishing the man would get to the point and hang up. He had other things to worry about. Such as how to reopen the lines of communication with Addy.

"Well, I wouldn't have bothered you—" Blandings sounded as if he wished he hadn't "—but you did tell me that I was to call you at once if I was able to buy up that loan that David Edwards took out on the factory last winter. We were able to get it for fifty cents on the dollar because it's three weeks overdue and the investor is worried that Edwards will default on it. The grace period will be up on the sixth."

Joe waited for the surge of pleasure he'd expected at the news that he now had the means to tighten the net around Edwards to the point where it would strangle him. It didn't come. He probed deeper. The pleasure was there, but it was a pale shadow of what he'd expected. He was too concerned with the problem of Addy, he rationalized. Once he had things back on an even keel with her, then he'd be able to appreciate what Blandings was telling him.

"Thank you for letting me know," Joe finally said. "I'll be in touch with you shortly about what I want to do with it."

"Certainly. I hope you're feeling better."

"I—" Joe tensed as the doorbell suddenly rang. Addy! It had to be Addy. Anyone else would have activated his alarm system when they opened the gate onto the grounds. And someone climbing over the fence would hardly be ringing his doorbell.

"Mr. Barrington?" Blandings's perplexed voice sounded from the phone. Joe stared at it, surprised to find the connection still open.

"Sorry, I'll talk to you later," he said, and slammed the phone down. He hurried toward the door, mentally scrambling for an approach. He hadn't found one when he flung it open.

Addy forced herself to meet his gaze even though it was one of the hardest things she'd ever done. Everything depended on her playing it cool, she reminded herself. This wasn't the time for emotion. She could wallow later. Now she needed to have all her wits about her if she was going to be able to salvage something from last night's fiasco.

"I..." To her dismay her voice cracked. She firmed it and plowed on. "I wanted to make sure that you had recovered from your bout with the flu," she said, forcing out the excuse she'd decided on.

"I'm fine," Joe muttered. "It was just a twenty-four-hour thing."

"Well, that's good." Addy scrambled to think of something to add to prolong the conversation.

"Yes, I have a full week, and it wouldn't do to be sick." Joe listened to his inane chatter with a feeling of disbelief. How could he be blathering about how he felt when what was important was how *she* felt. He studied her hungrily, noting the paleness of her skin and the tightness around her mouth. She looked upset, but even so she hadn't flatly rejected him. She had come to see how he was. Maybe his best bet would be to pretend that yesterday had never happened. That he had never held her naked body in his arms while they both writhed in ecstasy. Or, at least, try to. He doubted he'd ever really forget what had happened. It was burned into his soul.

"Come in." He stepped out of the doorway and gestured inside hoping she'd come. "I was just about to have a cup of coffee."

Addy felt light-headed with relief at his invitation. He wasn't going to shut her out of his life. He was going to treat her exactly as he had before. A feeling of pique followed on the heels of the relief, but she told herself not to be ridiculous. This way, she could at least enjoy his company.

"Have you had anything to eat today?" She eyed him worriedly, not liking the grayish tinge to his skin.

"Food?" Joe parroted as if it were an alien concept he hadn't encountered before.

"As in nourishment?"

"I'm not hungry."

"Eat anyway," she ordered. "Your body needs the energy. Come on. I'll scramble you a couple of eggs."

Joe followed her out to the kitchen. He wasn't the slightest bit hungry, but he was so grateful to have their relationship back to something approaching normal that he'd have eaten anything she wanted him to. He perched on a stool at the breakfast bar and watched her as she deftly fixed him some eggs and added a couple of pieces of toast.

"Eat," Addy ordered as she set the plate down in front of him. She poured them both a cup of coffee and, leaning up against the counter, surreptitiously watched him. Now what? she wondered. What could she do to reinforce their tentative accord?

If he thought she was still actively looking for a husband,

it might put to rest any lingering doubts he had about her wanting to marry him, she finally decided.

"If you're not busy on Saturday night, there's a concert in the park that I thought we could go to," Addy said. "It would be good practice for me for relating to a man in a crowd."

Joe stared down at his eggs, feeling queasy at the thought of Addy dating another man. It was for the best, he tried to tell himself, because with Addy there was no middle ground. She'd never agree to an affair with him until what they felt for each other had burned itself out. With those damned inconvenient morals of hers, she'd want a commitment. Promises of forever after and priests throwing holy water at them.

What did he feel for her? The unexpected question popped up in his mind. He studied her out of the corner of his eye. His gaze automatically drifted down the length of her body, and his palms itched as he remembered the feel of her soft breasts in his hands. He desired her, he thought, but it was more than that. What he felt was stronger than mere desire. He lusted after her. Lusted after her with an intensity that he hadn't even realized he could feel. But why?

He absently chewed on his toast as he considered the problem. Addy certainly wasn't the most beautiful woman he knew. Nor was her body the most perfect. But when added together with the vitality of her personality and the sharpness of her mind, the effect on him was unprecedented. Maybe it was because he knew her better than he had ever known a woman before? And not only did he lust after her, but he admired her, too, he realized. He admired her sense of ethics, which wasn't swayed by popular opinion. And he admired the fact that she was willing to put herself out for her own beliefs. Like that clinic she'd nagged him into letting her establish in the plant.

Addy broke into his thoughts. "On the other hand, if you're too busy to take me, it doesn't matter."

Joe stared blankly at her, having lost the train of their conversation. "What are you talking about?"

"I asked you to take me to the concert Saturday. Are you sure you're all right?"

"I didn't get much sleep last night," he muttered, seizing the first excuse that came into his mind, and then wished he hadn't when he saw the flush stain her cheeks.

"But I'll take you...." he started to say, then paused as his normal sense of caution kicked in. "What are they playing? Not some of that New Age stuff that sounds like random chords being struck by a cranky class of kindergartners?"

"New Age music does not sound random. At least, not most of it," she added fairly. "But you can rest easy. They're playing Sousa marches and ending with the 1812 Overture."

Joe's eyes lit up in sudden interest. "Are they going to fire the old Civil War cannon by the bandstand during the finale?"

"I hope not," Addy said, feeling the tight hard cord of tension deep within her start to relax. "All the men will be hanging around it like a bunch of kids, and someone is bound to get hurt. Finish your eggs."

"Did anyone ever tell you that you're bossy?"

Addy grinned at him. "No, they didn't have the nerve."

Joe focused on the upward curve of her lips. He wanted to kiss her. He needed to kiss her. The compulsion was fast reaching uncontrollable proportions. He risked a glance up into her brown eyes, fascinated by the sparkling light he could see reflected there. He really should kiss her, he reasoned, because if he suddenly stopped kissing her, she'd think that he was doing it because of their having made love. She'd think that he attached more importance to what had happened than was normal.

Everyone kissed, he rationalized. Women he barely knew threw their arms around him and kissed him. It didn't mean anything more than shaking someone's hand meant. And

Addy hadn't minded before. Would she mind now that he'd made love to her? He didn't know. All he knew was that he had to find out.

Just keep it casual, he encouraged himself. Leave yourself room to retreat without losing face if she slaps you down.

"No one in his right mind would be scared of you," he scoffed. "Even if you forgot yourself to the extent of yelling at someone, you'd immediately start to worry that you'd damaged their self-esteem."

Addy frowned at him. "You make me sound like a goody-two-shoes."

"No," Joe said softly. "I make you sound like a woman is supposed to be."

"I'm not sure, but I have a feeling that comment was horribly sexist."

"See what you think about this," he murmured and, leaning forward, lightly brushed his lips across her soft mouth. Sparks skittered over his skin, lighting little fires of need where they landed. The scent of her perfume teased his mind with images of warm summer days and fields of fragrant flowers basking under a bright sun. He needed more than this, he thought hungrily. Needed it to restore some semblance of normalcy to his off-kilter world.

He tentatively slipped his arms around her and then lightly rested his mouth against hers. An overwhelming feeling of relief chased through him when Addy made no effort to repulse him. Cautiously deciding to try to deepen the kiss, he gently tugged her closer between his spread legs.

His heart began to thud at the feel of her pressed between his inner thighs and a longing for more slammed through him. He indulged himself to the extent of allowing his hands to slip lower so that he could cup her hips. His fingers pressed into her soft flesh and he lifted her slightly, pulling her into the cradle of his hips. Pleasure rocked through him as his body began to respond to her closeness.

He needed to taste her. To make love to her. No! Joe determinedly shut off that line of thought and pulled back. That was how he'd got into this mess in the first place, by indulging his needs.

Addy took a deep breath, her eyes focused on the firm line of his lips. Although she wanted a lot more than he'd just given her, she still felt good. Somehow, she'd managed to diffuse most of the tension from what had happened last night. Now, if she could just keep his focus on other things...

"I'll have to get myself another kitchen chair." She said the first thing that popped into her head. "That way you can eat at my place, too."

"Go look in the attic if you want a chair."

"You keep kitchen chairs in the attic?"

"When I bought this place, it was semifurnished. I had the contractor dump all the furniture up in the attic, and as far as I know it's all still there. You can have anything you want."

"I'll go see while you finish your breakfast." Addy headed for the back stairs. Not only was she curious about what might be up there, but poking through his attic would give her a chance to regain her equilibrium after that tantalizing kiss he'd given her. She hugged herself in a sudden burst of pleasure. Things had worked out far better than she'd dared hope.

Addy blinked as she pushed open the attic door and found stacks of boxes and furniture that stretched to the back wall. "Wow," she muttered, looking around her in disbelief. It looked like a gigantic rummage sale. And Joe had said that she could have anything she wanted.

Cautiously, she made her way through the stacks, looking for something promising. Most of the furniture consisted of massive pieces of heavy, dark oak that would need a large room to balance them. But toward the back of the attic she did find a delicate-looking spindle chair and, as she was carefully maneuvering it toward the door, she discovered a small, square footlocker that she could use as a bedside table.

She set the chair down, put the footlocker on top of it and carefully carried them downstairs.

She found Joe in the living room reading *The Wall Street Journal*. Addy paused for a moment in the doorway and feasted her eyes on him, savoring the slightly rumpled look of his dark hair. She wanted nothing so much as to run her fingers through it and further dishevel it. To sit down in his lap and explore every inch of his face with her lips.

Addy swallowed, determinedly pushing down the impulse. She needed to go slowly. To follow his lead and, at the moment, his interest seemed to be firmly focused on his paper.

"Did you finish your eggs?" Addy asked.

"They're all gone."

Which wasn't the same thing at all as eating them. Addy examined his phrasing. What he'd said would be true even if he had scraped them down the garbage disposal. Mentally, she sighed. He was a grown man. If he didn't want to eat, she couldn't make him.

Unconsciously her eyes drifted down the length of his body, studying on the width of his chest before slowly allowing her eyes to linger on the flatness of his stomach. A very grown man. A shiver of remembered bliss chased over her skin, and she ran her tongue over her lower lip. Down, girl, she counseled herself.

"What'd you find?" Joe gestured toward the footlocker.

Addy picked up the footlocker to show him and felt something move inside it.

"I wanted to use it as a bedside table to hold my alarm clock, but there's something in it."

"No problem, dump it out."

"But it might belong to someone."

Joe shook his head. "Not to anyone that's going to object. It was part of the stuff that I moved out of the attic of my grandmother's house when my mother died. It's been in storage ever since."

Curious about what was in it, Addy tried to open it, but the lock refused to budge. She wiggled it and when that didn't work, smacked it with her palm.

Joe snorted in disgust at her efforts. "Here. Let me."

Addy handed him the footlocker and watched as he took a metal paper clip off a sheath of papers sitting on the end table, unbent it and inserted one end into the lock.

"You have unexpected talents," she said approvingly.

Joe grinned at her. "You haven't seen anything yet."

Addy felt a fiery flush stain her cheeks as the memory of just what she had seen so far flooded her mind. With a little luck she might get him back into bed again. But right now she needed to stifle her burgeoning desires. First, Joe needed time to recover from his bout with the flu as well as to let his fears of being trapped into some kind of commitment abate. Then, perhaps…

An audible snick interrupted her delightful plans, and she glanced down. Joe had the lock open.

"Done." Joe gestured toward the footlocker in satisfaction. "It's all yours."

Opening the lid, she peered in. There were two neat stacks of cancelled checks inside. Addy picked up one stack and looked at it. It was made out to Catherine Barrington and was for the sum of two thousand dollars. Addy flipped through the stack to discover that they were identical. All were made out to Joe's mother and all were for the sum of two thousand dollars. The only difference was the dates. They had been written on the first of each month over a period of years. Many years, Addy realized as she picked up the second stack and checked the date at the bottom of the pile. The first check had been written over thirty years ago. In fact… She turned to Joe and stared speculatively at him.

"How old are you?" she asked.

"Thirty-six."

"I know that. I meant when is your birthday?"

"June 29th, why?"

Addy squinted into the distance as she made the calculations. The checks had started three months before Joe had been born and had continued—she checked the last date—right up until his mother had died. Why?

"What did you find?" Joe took one of the stacks out of her hand and stared at it. His expression darkened as he flipped through the stack.

"What the hell!" he muttered.

"I would say that was how your mother was able to pay the bills all those years without working," Addy said.

"But why would—" Joe checked the signature on the checks "—Francis Layton be writing checks to my mother?"

"Could he actually be your father?" Addy suggested uncertainly.

Joe shook his head. "Mom was very specific about Edwards. Besides, I told you. I went to see the old bastard and he admitted it."

"I can't ever remember knowing anyone named Layton," she said. "Can you?"

"The name doesn't ring a bell, but the signature on the back is Mom's," he conceded.

Addy's heart twisted at the confusion in his eyes. Perhaps this was what was needed to get Joe to finally face the fact that his mother was a human being with faults just like the rest of them. If he could do that, then perhaps he could finally begin to see his father as something other than the devil incarnate. Which just might lead to him dropping his vendetta against his half brother. And if he could do that, then perhaps he would finally be free to grow emotionally. Addy followed her line of reasoning through to its logical conclusion. Grow in her direction? She could only hope.

"Do you have a telephone book?" she asked.

"In there." Joe gestured toward an end-table drawer.

Addy got it out and, opening it to the Ls, looked for Layton.

"Eureka! There is a Francis Layton listed." She peered closer. "It says he's an attorney. With offices downtown." Addy slammed the book shut and got her feet. The sooner they confronted Layton the better.

"Where are you going?" Joe asked.

"*We* are going downtown to see Layton."

"See him?" Joe stared at her as a feeling of unease skittered through his mind.

"You want to find out why he wrote checks to your mother for over twenty-eight years, don't you?"

Did he? Joe wondered. Did he really want to investigate this latest development? He shivered, feeling strangely uncertain.

"But Mom never had any money," he muttered. "She could never afford to buy me the kind of toys the other kids had, or pay for summer camp or…"

"She had the money to buy liquor," Addy said, pointing out the obvious.

Joe automatically leapt to her defense. "Mom needed the alcohol to…"

"To what? To face life? Why was her life so horrible? She had you. She had a mother who loved her. She had job skills. She had her health. At least, she did until she drowned it in alcohol."

"You don't understand! She lost the man she loved. The man she trusted."

Addy suppressed a flicker of sympathy for the dead Catherine. She really did understand how devastated she must have felt when Edwards had said that it was over. She understood because that was the way she felt about Joe. If she could no longer see him… But even so, Addy didn't think that she'd take refuge in a bottle. Not if she had had a child. She'd want to take care of the child.

"Granted your mother took a hard knock," Addy said slowly, "but even you must admit that it wasn't quite as hard as she would have had you believe." She gestured toward the canceled checks.

"There has to be an explanation for them," Joe muttered, feeling as if the foundations of his life were shifting.

"Well, whatever it is, we aren't going to find it by sitting here," Addy said, to drive her point home. "Layton is the key to this."

"But—"

"Unless you're afraid to find out the truth!" Addy gibed, trying to force him to act.

Joe glared at her. "If that crack is supposed to motivate me to go charging off to see Layton..."

Addy let out her breath in a long sigh. Trust Joe to see through her attempt at psychological manipulation. "Actually it was," she admitted candidly. "I couldn't think of any other way to make you face your fears."

"I am not afraid!"

Addy shrugged.

"Oh, hell!" he muttered. "You won't be happy until we've seen this Layton character and gotten the whole sordid story out of him. Come on." He stalked toward the door.

Addy grabbed a couple of the checks and hurried after him, madly hoping that she was doing the right thing.

Nine

Addy ran her finger down the list of tenants in the professional building. "There." She pointed to Layton's name. "He's on the sixth floor."

She glanced sideways at Joe. He looked pale, paler than even having had the flu would account for. Maybe she was pushing too hard? But if not now, when? Quit dithering and get on with it, she ordered herself. She hurried over to the elevator as the doors opened.

Joe got in after her and jabbed the button for the sixth floor with far more vigor than was necessary.

Addy bit back the urge to fill the oppressive silence with chatter, and stared at the panel on the elevator beside the doors.

Finally, after what seemed like hours to her overstretched nerves, the elevator stopped with a slight hiccup on the sixth floor and the doors opened. Addy got out and began checking the names on the offices. She found Layton's office three suites down and, opening the door, entered.

Curious, she looked around. The office radiated good taste, money and stability.

"Old-line family firm," Joe's muttered assessment agreed with hers.

"May I help...you?"

Addy watched in annoyance as the receptionist's eyes widened as if she couldn't believe what fate had just thrown her way. Addy inched closer to Joe.

"We'd like to see Mr. Layton," Addy finally said when Joe remained silent as if divorcing himself from what was happening.

"Do you have an appointment?" the woman asked.

"No, but we still need to see him," Addy persisted.

"And what name should I give him?"

"J. E. Barrington." Addy used Joe's name in the hopes that it would prove more potent at opening doors than hers would.

To her relief, it did. The receptionist disappeared into an office, and returned a moment later with an invitation to go into the law library. She added that Mr. Layton would be with them just as soon as he got off the phone.

Addy followed the woman into the library and sank down on the leather sofa to wait. To her pleasure, Joe choose to sit beside her. Close beside her. She could feel the tension vibrating through his body.

"Ah, Mr. Barrington." An immaculately groomed man in his early forties hurried in through the door behind them. "I'm very pleased to meet you, and..." He studied Addy with a curiosity that she didn't find offensive.

"Miss Edson," Joe introduced her.

Addy studied Layton as she shook his hand. This couldn't be the Layton who had signed those early checks. He would have still been a child at the time.

Apparently the same thing had occurred to Joe, because he asked, "I rather think it's your father we want to see."

The man smiled sadly at him. "Unfortunately, Dad suffers from Alzheimer's and is in a nursing home. Even if you went out to see him, I doubt you'd get much sense from him. But if there is any way that I can help you..."

"You could tell me what the hell is going on!" Joe bit out.

"Going on?" Layton responded cautiously.

"We'd like an explanation of these." Addy pulled one of the checks she'd brought along out of her pocket and handed it to him.

Layton looked at it as if it were a snake that might bite him and said, "I didn't realize that my father had sent the canceled checks back to her."

"Then you do know about them?" Addy pounced.

"Yes, I know, although I was little more than a child when it was all set up. And I have a problem here with client confidentiality—"

"You're going to have a far bigger problem with me if you don't tell me what this is all about." Joe's voice sent a shiver up Addy's spine. He sounded absolutely ruthless. Not at all the kind of man one would want to make an enemy of.

Apparently Layton felt the same way, for he tugged ineffectively on his tie and muttered, "I guess it would be all right. I mean, the other interested parties are all dead. And poor Dad will never know." Then he took a deep breath and said, "What is it you want to know?"

"These checks were actually cashed?" Joe demanded.

"Oh, yes," Layton assured him. "We hand-delivered them on the first of every month and your mother would cash them, usually the same day."

"Who was your father acting for?" Joe continued.

"Andrew Edwards," Layton said.

"So he did pay." Joe turned and walked over to the window, where he stood staring down into the street below. His shoulders were braced as if he couldn't bear the weight of what he'd just heard.

"Yes, he paid." Layton treated the comment as a question. "Mr. Edwards had...how shall I put it? An unfortunate propensity for extramarital affairs. Although to the best of my knowledge, you were the only…''

''Bastard.'' Joe's harsh voice tore at Addy's heart. ''I'm surprised that he was willing to support me.''

Layton rubbed his finger along the bridge of his nose. ''From what my father said, he didn't have much choice. He was afraid that your mother would go to his wife if he didn't.''

Addy frowned, seeing the flaw in the logic. ''But it seems to me that if that was his concern, he'd only make Catherine's case stronger by giving her money.''

''Yes, well… Mr. Edwards took care of that eventuality.''

Joe turned around and gave him a cold look. ''Do tell us what Mr. Edwards's solution to the problem was.''

Layton swallowed audibly. ''He had a cousin about his own age who was in the service. He was sent to Vietnam about that time and killed there almost immediately. Edwards had your mother sign a paper saying that his cousin was your father in exchange for the monthly support payment and your college fees.''

''Which would make it impossible to prove who Joe's father was with a DNA test,'' Addy finished.

''Do you mean to tell me that he paid for my college fees?'' Joe demanded.

Layton looked puzzled. ''Of course. Why shouldn't he have? You were his son. In fact, you're far more like him than David ever was.''

''I am not!'' Joe's hands clenched into fists with the strength of his rejection of the idea, and Layton instinctively stepped back a pace.

''Thank you for your information, Mr. Layton.'' Addy saw no value in prolonging the discussion.

Layton shrugged. ''It was the least I could do, Miss Edson. I know Dad was never happy about the whole business, but anyone who knew anything about Edwards knew that he'd never give up the company, which was what acknowledging Mr. Barrington as his son would have cost him. And this way, at least, Catherine had the money to raise him.''

Even if she didn't use it for that, Joe thought bitterly as he stalked out of the office without another word. He felt as if his guts had been ripped loose. As if he were swinging wildly around in a world that had no firm anchors left anywhere.

Addy hurried after him, worried about his set, tense expression. Tentatively, she touched his arm as he stepped into the elevator, but before she could say anything a woman and her three kids hurried in after them. She knew that she would have to wait—at least until they were in the car—to talk to him.

Addy swallowed nervously as he backed his car out of the parking space with a controlled ferocity that frightened her. She'd wanted Joe to face the past, but she hadn't quite expected it to bother him so much. She stifled a sigh. The problem was that Joe was a very complex person. You never knew how he was going to react, especially when you were dealing with his emotions, because he didn't seem to have a very good handle on them.

"Joe."

"What?" He bit the word out.

"I don't know what," she said honestly.

"All those years," he muttered as if he hadn't heard her. "The whole time I was growing up, I wore castoffs that the minister's wife down the street would pass along to me. I never had a new pair of shoes or a bike like the other kids until I finally got a newspaper route when I was eleven. 'We have no money,' she'd say. 'I can barely keep us in food. Don't eat so much.' And all the time she had a better income than most of our neighbors. Why?" The word seemed torn out of him. "Why wasn't I worth taking care of?"

"It didn't have anything to do with you." Addy grabbed the door handle as he accelerated around a curve. "It had to do with your mother's addiction. Addicts don't think about how their actions are affecting the people around them. All they care about is getting the next high.''

"She was my mother, dammit! If she'd loved me, she would have spent some money on me.''

Addy winced at the pain in his voice. She wanted desperately to wrap her arms around him and tell him that it didn't matter what his mother had felt, because she loved him enough to make up for anything. But she couldn't. He didn't want to hear that. A depressing weight seemed to press her down against the soft leather of his car seat.

"Joe...'' She fumbled to find the right words.

"Spare me the platitudes about it not really being her fault!''

"You make me want to give you a good swift smack upside the head,'' she snapped, deciding that since sympathy wasn't working, maybe the plain, unvarnished truth would. "What I can't figure out is how you ever managed to make a go of your business. You don't think. First, you view your mother as a victim. Now you find out that she had an income all those years, you do an about-face and decide she's a villain.''

"What would you call a woman who deprived her kid of necessities to buy alcohol?'' he asked bitterly.

"A very weak person,'' Addy said. "For whatever reason, your mother did not have the inner resources to deal with life as it was and not as she wanted it to be. Actually, the wonder is that you are as strong a person as you are.''

"Someone had to be,'' he muttered.

And the someone in this case had been a small boy struggling against overwhelming odds. Addy felt her heart twist with love.

"If it hadn't been for your mother being so weak, you might not have turned out the way you did,'' she pointed out. "If you had had a normal childhood, you probably wouldn't be where you are today.''

"Oh, so now you want me to be grateful to her?" he sneered.

Addy swallowed on her sense of frustration. "No, I want you to act like an adult. To admit that your mother was a human being with problems. Problems that led her to make choices that weren't good for you. For that matter, they were worse for her. She'd still be alive today if she hadn't drunk like that."

"It's easy enough for you to say."

Addy studied the corded muscles showing in his jaw as he turned the car into his driveway. Joe was right about one thing. It was a lot easier for her to say than it was for him to believe. He needed to mull over what he'd learned. To let it sink in and come to grips with it before he could forgive his mother for the mess she'd made of his childhood.

She decided to change the subject. "Now that I've got a chair, do you want to come for dinner?"

Joe glanced over at her. No, he didn't want to eat dinner with her. He wanted to make love to her; he allowed his need to coalesce into a single, coherent thought. He wanted to gather her soft body against him and absorb her into him. He wanted to luxuriate in the feel of her hot, pulsating flesh contracting around him. He wanted to sate himself in her and obliterate the pain of what he'd just discovered. But he couldn't.

Or could he? He parked in front of the cottage. Addy was an adult, and it wasn't as if he was lying to her, making a lot of promises about being in love with her and them living happily ever after. If she didn't want him to go to bed with her, she could say so.

He could feel some of his angry tension start to seep out of him just at the thought of being able to hold her. Even if she wouldn't go to bed with him, she might let him kiss her. And he'd rather kiss Addy than make love to anyone else.

"I'll let you pick the menu." Addy tried to keep her

voice light when he didn't answer her. She'd known making him face the truth about the past was a risk, but if the price she was going to have to pay was to lose him... A shiver of despair slithered over her skin.

"I'm not hungry," he said, "but..." He paused, trying to figure out how to ask her if she would like to go to bed with him. It seemed unlikely, especially considering the mess he'd made of things the last time. But he felt so alone. He shivered from the cold that seemed lodged in his stomach. He needed her. Needed her to feel whole again.

"But?" she asked.

He looked into Addy's soft brown eyes and felt his guts twist with longing.

"But I'd like a cup of coffee," he finally said. He couldn't ask her without some kind of buildup, he rationalized. He'd drink coffee and talk to her and then he'd take her in his arms and kiss her and... He swallowed as his body began to react.

"I have some cookies, too." Addy felt herself relax at his words. He wasn't going to shut her out for the part she'd played in his discovery.

Joe followed her into the cottage. He wandered around the living room, picking up things and putting them down while Addy watched him, wanting to make everything right, but knowing that she couldn't. Only Joe could come to terms with his memories.

Probably her best bet would be to try to pretend that this afternoon had never happened, at least until he brought the subject up again. If he ever did. She'd treat him exactly as she had before, she decided as she went into the kitchen to make instant coffee. Mentally, she made a note to buy a coffee maker.

She knew how she'd like to treat him, she thought dreamily as she got out the saucepan she used to heat water and filled it. As a dearly beloved man. She'd like to be able to touch him anytime she wanted. In any way she wanted.

"Why are you letting the water run over that pan?" Joe's

curious voice brought her back to earth with a thud. Hastily, she turned off the faucet and emptied some of the water out of the pan before setting it on the stove.

"I was thinking," she muttered.

"Your problem is, you think too much." He leaned against the counter and studied her.

Addy considered his comment, wondering what he meant. But she didn't want to know badly enough to ask. It sounded to her like the prelude to an argument, and she didn't want to fight with him. She just wanted to savor the pleasure of his company. And to do that she needed a subject to discuss that wasn't fraught with emotional pitfalls. Unfortunately, everything about Joe was fraught with emotional pitfalls. She only had to look at him, and she became a boiling mass of emotional need.

"I'm going to hold my first baby clinic next Friday," she finally offered.

"I know. One of the men in production was complaining about it to personnel."

Addy frowned. "Why would he complain? It's free, and it's noncompulsory."

"He complained because he doesn't have any young kids, and he does have high blood pressure. He claims that the company's discriminating against his particular ailment in favor of kids. Or as he said, 'a squalling bunch of brats.'"

"But I haven't had anything to do with adult hypertension since I was a student nurse. If he's been doing any reading about it at all, he has to know as much as I do."

"I didn't say his complaint was logical, just that he made one. He's going to file it with the union."

Addy winced. "Can he make trouble?"

Joe shrugged. "I doubt it. The shop steward's wife just had twins."

Addy chuckled. "Good. But you know the man might have a point," she said slowly. "Perhaps you could invite various health professionals to speak on different subjects. Like hypertension and diabetes and—''

''Mental health? My own comes to mind.''

''Nonsense. The healthier your workforce is, the cheaper it is for an employer.''

''Let's see how the baby clinic works out before we begin expanding,'' Joe hedged.

Addy nodded, and turned to make their coffee. Joe had a point about not tackling too much at once, but even so it was an intriguing idea. His plant would be a great place to try out a lot of her ideas on health care. Absently, she picked up the pan to pour the boiling water into the mugs. To her shock the handle was hot and she instinctively jerked, splashing boiling water all down the front of her.

''Augh!'' Addy flung the pan in the sink and ineffectively plucked at her steaming T-shirt.

''Get that off before it scalds you!'' Not waiting to see if she obeyed, Joe grabbed the hem of her shirt and yanked it over her head, then hurriedly stripped off her wet bra.

Addy instinctively tried to cover herself with her hands. She might love Joe to distraction, but she was still too unsure of herself to allow him to look at her bare body in the clear, cold light of day.

Joe barely noticed. His whole focus was on what she had done to herself. He jerked opened the snap on her jeans and reached for the zipper.

''No!'' Addy pushed his hands away.

''What the hell do you mean, no? That water was boiling. You have to get out of those clothes. Now.'' He wrenched the zipper down.

''Don't!'' Addy wailed.

''For God's sake, woman, I'm not trying to rape you.''

The hurt expression in Joe's eyes tore at Addy's soft heart. It was unthinkable that he feel that she was afraid of him. Or that she didn't like his advances. If the price of easing his hurt was the truth...

Addy took a deep breath and blurted out, "I can't take off my clothes because you'll see my stretch marks."

"Stretch marks!" he repeated incredulously. "I'm worried about your being scalded, and you're blathering about stretch marks?"

"Yes," she muttered. "When I lost all that weight, it left stretch marks."

"I think you lost your mind, too," he grumbled. "Either you take them off or I will."

Addy slowly put her hands on the waistband, knowing he was right about getting out of them, but still not wanting to do it.

Losing patience, Joe batted her hands away and yanked her jeans and panties off.

Addy bit back an embarrassed moan. She wanted to run and hide in the closet, but two things stopped her: the fear that Joe would take her flight personally and the fact that he might decide that she was too emotionally immature to ever make love to again.

It was too bad that she hadn't been born back in Victorian times, she thought grimly. Back when everything was done at night under the covers.

"Your skin's red!" The sharp concern in Joe's voice was a balm to her frazzled nerves. "Does it hurt?"

"Not much," Addy answered truthfully. Her mind was too busy trying to deal with the sensation his wandering fingers were causing to worry about anything as inconsequential as a few burns.

"What stretch marks?"

Addy looked down into his face. Her attention was snared by the gleaming points of light winking in and out of his eyes.

"I don't want to talk about it," she muttered, wondering how to get him off her less-than-perfect body and on to other things. Such as kissing her. Or better yet, making love to her.

Joe arched his dark brows in mock horror. "This from

the woman who told me I had to face the past and deal with it?''

"That's different!"

"Sure, that was me. This is you," he said dryly. "Anyway, you're making mountains out of molehills. I can't see any stretch marks.''

He leaned closer, and Addy felt the sensitive skin on her abdomen quiver as his breath warmed it. She stared down at the top of his gleaming black hair. This was crazy, she thought in confusion. How did she come to be standing naked in her kitchen with Joe's head inches from her belly, looking for stretch marks? And purporting not to find them.

Could he really think they weren't all that noticeable? Or could it be that they simply weren't as important to him as they were to her? She didn't know, but whatever the reason, she was more than willing to accept it.

"Maybe it's a tactile thing," he murmured and, leaning forward, ran the tip of his tongue over her skin.

Addy jerked violently as a torrent of sensation slammed through her. All of a sudden her bones felt rubbery, and she wavered slightly.

To her surprise, Joe scooped her up in his arms and carried her into the living room, where he sat down on the sofa with her in his lap.

Addy snuggled her face into his chest as much in embarrassment at being naked while he was fully dressed as from a desire to be close to him. He shifted her slightly, fitting her more closely against him, and she relished the ripple of his supple muscles as he moved. He smelled so good, she thought dreamily. So masculine.

She wanted him to kiss her. To make love to her. Even though she knew that it would end in pain, she still wanted it. The sense of sharing and the euphoric pleasure that preceded the pain was worth it. But what did Joe want? She barely suppressed a shudder as she remembered his reaction to the last time they'd made love. He hadn't meant to do it then, so there was no reason that he might want to do it now.

"Maybe I should take you to the hospital?" He sounded worried.

"No," she said hastily. Leaving the house did not fit into her plans. "I was just dizzy there for a second. Shock more than anything else. I'll get dressed," she said, making a halfhearted effort to get up.

"Stay here for a minute while you rest," Joe ordered. "Then we'll consider what we should do about your red marks."

He gently traced around the edge of the one on her abdomen. The slightly roughened skin of his fingers sent shivers spiraling through her.

Addy sucked her breath in with an audible gasp as her skin quivered in reaction to his fleeting touch.

"Was that painful?" Joe demanded.

"Not exactly," Addy muttered, wondering how to get his mind off injuries and onto pleasures. She peeped up at him from beneath her lashes. His features looked tense, but she didn't think it was with sexual tension. How could she hint what she wanted without coming right out and saying so? She simply didn't feel secure enough in their strange relationship to actually ask. No, she amended, it wasn't the asking that bothered her. It was the thought of trying to deal with the humiliation if he should refuse.

"Why don't you kiss it and make it better?" Addy finally said. Surely that would give him a clue to what she wanted and if he didn't share her mood, he could simply give her a quick kiss and that way she could retreat without losing face.

Joe's eyes widened, and he stared down at her as if weighing her words. "Kiss it and make it better?" he repeated cautiously.

"That's the time-honored cure, I believe." She forced the words out. She squirmed nervously and her bare buttocks scraped across the rough material of his slacks. A voluptuous feeling raced along her nerve endings and she tensed, trying hard not to move. Not to do anything that might distract him from what she wanted.

"Far be it from me to mess with tradition," Joe said. "If you're sure?" It seemed to Addy that there were nuances in his voice that she didn't begin to understand. A fact which really didn't surprise her. Joe was a very complex man, and she didn't really understand a great deal of his personality. Not that she wasn't eager to learn more.

Addy took a deep breath and said, "I'm sure."

For a second, his arms tightened convulsively around her and then he stood, laying her back on the sofa. The sleek velvet of the sofa's cushions caressed her bare back, seeming to sensitize her skin. Addy closed her eyes the better to savor the feeling and, when she opened them, it was to see Joe hurriedly yanking off his clothes. He didn't even seem to notice when a button from his shirt went flying.

His unabashed haste fed her fragile self-confidence. Joe was as eager to make love to her as she was to make love to him. Addy's eyes widened as he kicked off his slacks and she saw just exactly how eager he was.

Lured by his blatant masculinity, Addy reached out and lightly brushed her fingertips against his thigh. His dark hair felt rough. Rough and very exciting. She pressed slightly, but there was almost no give to his thighs. They were solid muscle.

"Your body feels so different from mine," she said slowly. "So hard and—"

Joe's deep chuckle sent a flush over her cheeks.

"*Vive la différence,*" he quoted as he dropped to his knees beside the couch. "Now, as I remember it, I was supposed to be giving you first aid."

Addy ran her tongue over her suddenly dry lips as he leaned toward her. The warmth of his breath made the tender skin on her abdomen flutter, and she tensed in anticipation as he came closer.

When his lips finally touched her, Addy jerked at the hot shard of sensation that shot through her.

"You have the most fantastic skin," Joe murmured as he dragged his lips over her belly. "So incredibly soft and satiny and you always smell like flowers. The late-summer ones that used to grow in our neighbor's yard when I was a kid. I could spend all day doing this."

Addy locked her trembling muscles against the onslaught of feeling that his wandering lips were causing. He might be able to do this all day, but she sure couldn't. A bit more and she was likely to go stark, raving mad.

She gasped as his tongue darted out and began to paint a complicated design on her quivering flesh. His tongue felt hot. Burning hot. Hotter than the water that had scalded her.

"Joe!" She grabbed for his head, not sure exactly what it was that she wanted. Only that she wanted to be more involved. She wanted an outlet for the emotions that were seething through her.

"Yes?" His voice sounded deeper. Deeper and harsher.

"Kiss me." Addy forgot her shyness in her need to satisfy the urgency that was building in her.

"I thought I was," he teased, but to her relief, he stretched out on the couch beside her and, slipping an arm beneath her shoulders, pulled her to him.

Addy trembled at the feel of his hard body pushing against her from shoulder to thigh. His chest hair scraped over the sensitive skin of her breasts, and she could feel them swelling in response. They felt heavy, taut with need. She wiggled slightly and her nipples convulsed into aching buds.

Her eyelids felt weighted with her burgeoning feelings. Deliberately, she tried to isolate the tantalizing sensations so that she could savor each individual one, but it was hopeless. The feelings continued to multiply, escalating to the point that she doubted her ability to contain them much longer.

Addy stared up at Joe. His eyes glittered with tiny chips of blue ice, and his face was hard, all sharp angles and unyielding planes.

Addy ran her tongue over her lower lip, mentally urging him to hurry up and kiss her. She shifted longingly, and a wave of jittery tremors chased over her as she felt his thrusting body.

Driven by a need that blinded her to other considerations, Addy finally clutched his head and pulled him down to her. His lips met hers with a sizzling impact, and for a long moment it was simply enough to feel the light pressure of his mouth. Then his lips pressed against hers and she suddenly wanted more. A lot more. She opened her mouth in silent invitation.

Quickly, Joe slid his tongue inside and began a slow, thorough exploration of her mouth.

Addy quivered as dancing shards of pleasure raced through her, making her feel dizzy and disoriented. Totally out of control. Wonderfully so. Deliberately, she allowed herself to sink deeper into the intoxicating sensations.

Shoving her fingers through his hair, she flexed them against his warm scalp. The faint aroma of his cologne hung in the superheated air between them, feeding the fires coursing through her as alcohol feeds a flame.

Her sense of urgency was building, building to the point where it was interfering with her motor coordination, making her reactions clumsy. Addy felt as if she were reaching for something, but as yet she couldn't tell exactly what her goal was. Only that Joe was the key. Only he could open the lock and set her free.

Addy moaned in denial when he lifted his head and broke their bond. He dropped a quick, hard kiss on her throbbing mouth and lowering his head, licked his tongue over the pebbly hard nub of her nipple.

Reaction crashed through her, collecting in her abdomen.

"Joe!" Addy gasped, having no idea what she wanted

to say. Only that she didn't want him to stop. Not ever. She felt as if she'd never be whole again if he did.

A high-pitched moan escaped through her tightly clenched teeth, as he took her nipple in his mouth and began to suckle it. Shivers chased over her skin, raising goose bumps as they passed.

She could hear the ragged sound of Joe's breathing echoing in her ears, adding to her sense of unreality. She felt as if she'd somehow stepped out of normal time and was suspended in a strange world where the normal rules of energy didn't apply. Where nothing had any reality except her feelings.

Addy felt a sense of loss as Joe's weight shifted off her, but before she could protest, he slipped between her legs. Addy's breath was blocked by the huge lump in her throat as she felt the hot, heavy length of him, pressing against her. For a moment, memory of the intense pain she'd felt last time intruded, dulling her sense of anticipation, but she refused to allow the memory to douse her pleasure. Determinedly, she tried to block it, focusing instead on the enticing feel of his hair-roughened legs pushing against the soft flesh of her inner thighs, of the pressure of his heavy body pushing her deeper into the velvety depths of the sofa's yielding cushions. She wanted this, she told herself. No matter how it ended, she still wanted it.

She stiffened as Joe slowly pushed forward, but to her surprise, the pain she felt this time was fleeting, gone almost before she realized that it was there. In its place was a scorching heat that flowed from his manhood to every cell of her body. Tentatively, almost afraid to believe what she was feeling, she arched upwards and was rewarded by a surge of pleasure.

A feeling of power and excitement welled within her. So this was what all the fuss was about. She opened her eyes slightly and stared up at him. His cheeks were darkly flushed, and his eyes burned with whatever inner vision he was seeing. The sunlight streaming in the window bathed him in a golden light, giving him a gleaming, ethereal quality. He looked like a being from another world—a far more interesting world than the one she normally inhabited.

Joe increased the tempo of his movement, and the tension gripping her suddenly increased a thousandfold. Increased to the point where nothing had any meaning expect Joe and the emotions he was creating. Pleasure wrapped itself around her in ever-tightening circles until she didn't think she could stand it any more. Her breath was coming in short, ragged gasps, and her body was so rigid she felt she might snap under the pressure. Finally, the escalating spiral snapped, hurtling her into a Technicolor world shot full of silvery sparkles that danced through her mind.

Addy barely noticed when Joe found his own release. It was only later, when she slowly drifted down through the clouds of sated feeling, that she realized he must have also experienced a reaction similar to hers, because she could think of no other explanation for the fact that he was lying bonelessly on top of her.

A secret smile of satisfaction curved her lips as she cradled him protectively against her.

"Too heavy," he muttered. She froze, for a moment catapulted back into her fat days.

"Squash you," he added, and deftly switched their positions. "There," he said. "Perfect."

"Perfect," Addy agreed, relaxing against him when she realized what he meant. As she should have known, she admitted. Joe would never be deliberately unkind to her.

He ran his fingers down her back, relishing the feel of her supple flesh beneath his fingers. He could feel every breath she drew and her soft breasts were a tantalizing weight on his chest. He felt totally relaxed in a way that he never had before. At peace with himself and the world. As if he could deal with anything. He sighed.

"What's wrong?" Addy asked.

"Nothing. I was just thinking what a wonderful thing friends are."

"Oh," Addy murmured, trying to be satisfied with the way he saw her. It wasn't what she wanted, but it sure beat nothing. And there was always the possibility that it might grow into something else, she encouraged herself.

She twitched as the phone rang, nuzzling her cheek against Joe's chest in negation of the sound, willing it to stop. When it didn't, she levered herself up and grabbed the receiver off the end table.

"Hello." She tried to keep her annoyance out of her voice.

"Hi, doll, this is Warren White," a self-satisfied voice informed her. "We kept missing each other this past weekend. I thought I'd pick you up about eight, and we could paint the town red."

Doll? Paint the town red? Addy grimaced. Didn't he know anything but clichés?

"Who is it?" Joe mouthed the words at her.

Addy covered the mouthpiece and whispered, "Warren White. He wants me to go out with him tonight."

Go out with him! Joe felt a gust of anger surge though him. How dare that overgrown Neanderthal try to move in on his Addy? It was clear all the guy wanted was to get her into bed. And she was too well-mannered to deal with the jerk the way he should be dealt with.

Joe grabbed the phone out of her hand. "This is Barrington. Listen up, White, because I'm only going to say this once. Stay away from Addy. Do I make myself clear?"

"Hell, man, if you'd told me you had something going with her in the first place..." Warren blustered.

Joe didn't listen. He simply slammed the phone down and pulled Addy back into his arms. She snuggled against him, but his sense of peace had been shattered.

"Stay away from that jerk," he ordered. "He's bad news."

"At least he's news." Addy felt that she should make some effort to keep alive the fiction that she was still looking for a husband. "The husband front is noted for being totally quiet."

"I don't care if it's deaf. Stay away from White. You need someone like…" He paused as he tried to think of someone that she could marry when the fervor of their affair had burned itself out. He couldn't. No one he knew was even nearly good enough for her. And not only that, but the thought of her making love to another man made his guts twist painfully. But Addy wanted a husband, he reminded himself. The only reason that she'd gotten involved with him in the first place was because he could help her capture one. If he didn't help her, she would probably leave. A shiver of loss chased over him. He couldn't decide which would be worse. Having her near, but not being able to make love to her, or not being able to see her at all.

Ten

Joe stared blankly down at the presentation he was supposed to be working on, totally unable to generate the slightest interest in the latest innovation in computer chips. Sooner or later and, if he knew Addy, it would be sooner rather than later, she was going to follow up on her idea that she should start dating other men. And, gut-wrenching as he found the idea, if he tried to stall too long she might go looking for someone on her own. And wind up with an egomaniac like White.

Dammit! He shoved the stack of papers aside in frustration, not even noticing when they fell onto his office floor. How could she even think of hunting for another man when what they were sharing was so wonderful? He grimaced at the obvious answer. Because she didn't find what they'd shared all that wonderful. Or maybe she simply didn't realize just how unusual their sexual affinity was. The only way she could find out would be to have sex with other men.

And even to prove the point, he didn't want her going

to bed with someone else. Not yet. Not until his burning
need for her had died and he was able to view her as just
an old friend. Unfortunately, he had no idea how long that
might take. It had been over a week since he'd first made
love to her and his need for her seemed to be growing, not
diminishing.

Which brought him back to his original problem. He
needed to find someone for her to date who wasn't going
to try to talk her into bed. Or, even worse, who might try
to marry her. His skin chilled at the thought. Once Addy
married, everything between them would be over. He knew
it with a certainty that made him numb. Once she made a
commitment to a man, she'd live by it. Even if she found
out that the sex wasn't anywhere near as good as it had
been with him.

Maybe he could hire someone to date Addy. He weighed
the idea. Someone that he could control. No, that wouldn't
work. Anyone unscrupulous enough to accept his offer
wasn't anyone he wanted around Addy. And even worse,
the guy might decide to marry Addy for her money. Between what she'd inherited from her parents, and what he
had paid her for the property, she had a nice sum invested.
More than enough to attract a fortune hunter.

The ringing of his phone broke into his fruitless thoughts.
Impatiently, he grabbed it and barked out, "Barrington."

"This is Blandings. Have I caught you at a bad time,
sir?"

Joe resisted the impulse to say yes and asked, "What's
up?"

"Well..." Blandings cleared his throat. "Yesterday was
the sixth, Mr. Barrington."

Which makes today the seventh, Joe thought impatiently.
How nice to know that for the outrageous fees he paid his
lawyer, he could get news flashes like that.

"And from the urgency with which you had originally
pursued the matter, I rather expected you to get in touch
with me yesterday."

Urgency? Joe frowned and then jerked up in his chair as

he suddenly realized what Blandings was talking about. The grace period on Edwards's overdue loan had passed yesterday. He could start foreclosure proceedings and finally get even with the family. He felt a surge of anticipation, which ebbed to leave unease in its wake. How could he possibly have forgotten the date? Even for a day? He'd waited so long for the chance to avenge his mother's wasted life.

Even if Addy was right and his mother had chosen to drink in response to Edwards ending their affair, it never would have happened if Edwards hadn't seduced her in the first place.

"Mr. Barrington?"

"Um, yes, I've been rather busy this week, but I certainly intend to continue with my original plan."

"I had the papers drawn up yesterday. Would you like me to serve them on Edwards?"

"No." Joe vetoed the idea. He wanted to be the one to give them to him. "Drop them off here at my office this afternoon. Then call Edwards and tell him that I want him to meet me at my house at six."

"Yes, Mr. Barrington. I'll take care of it."

Joe hung up and leaned back in his chair. He should be happier, he thought. In fact, he should be ecstatic. So why wasn't he?

"Oh, hell," he muttered. This business with Addy had him completely distracted. Maybe if he were to talk to her, he'd feel more like his normal self. He punched the number of her cottage into the phone, but there was no answer.

Maybe she was here at the clinic. He decided to walk over and see.

To his disappointment, Addy wasn't in the clinic. It was evident that she had been earlier in the day from the brilliantly colored posters she had hung everywhere, but of Addy there was no sign. Nor had the nurse been able to tell him where she was. Joe tried to stifle his sense of impatience, telling himself that he could talk to her when he got home that evening.

He was able to contain himself. Just. As it was, he left work half an hour earlier than he normally did. He took the shortcut home, parked his car in the garage and, picking up the foreclosure papers from the front seat, headed straight for Addy's cottage.

Addy leaned back on the couch and tried to relax her aching muscles. She'd spent the afternoon helping Kathy strip the wallpaper from her living room and in the process had discovered muscles she hadn't even been aware that she possessed.

She glanced over at the clock. The earliest she could reasonably expect to see Joe was five-thirty. She'd lie here for another half an hour, and then she'd go out front and pretend to be weeding the already immaculate flower beds in front of the cottage. Her lips curved in an anticipatory smile. That way, when Joe did come home she could intercept him. He'd undoubtedly stop to talk to her, and she could invite him for supper and... She shivered in anticipation.

Addy didn't know how long she had before he decided that he'd helped her enough, but one thing she was certain of was that she intended to cherish every minute. To savor the pleasure of his company and the wonder of his lovemaking because when it was gone...

A tight feeling of pain wrapped itself around her chest making it difficult to breathe. With a monumental effort, she dragged her thoughts away from the future. Given Joe's track record in maintaining relationships, the end would come all too soon. Which was all the more reason for her to live in the here and now while she had the opportunity. Because she had the nasty suspicion that in the days to come she was going to be spending a great deal of time living in the past.

Addy sat up at the brisk rap on her door, staring at it in surprise. Who could that be? It was too early for Joe. The knock sounded again, and Addy got to her feet to answer it, hoping it wasn't a friend come to renew an old acquaintance. Not that she didn't want to see old friends—she just didn't want to see them when there was the possibility that Joe might come.

Addy opened the door in the middle of the third knock, momentarily freezing under the strength of the pleasure that surged through her. Joe! He was early. Her eyes skimmed over the tailored perfection of his suit. And from the look of him, he'd come directly to see her. He hadn't even been up to the house to change.

"Have you been asleep?" Joe eyed her narrowly when she simply stood there.

"Asleep?" she muttered, distracted by the sight of him.

"Remember what happened to Sleeping Beauty." He leaned closer and the faint tang of his after-shave drifted toward her.

"Sleeping Beauty?" Addy parroted, her eyes focused on the mobile curve of his lips. "Are you referring to her eating the poisoned apple or her penchant for short, hairy men?"

Joe chuckled and his warm, faintly coffee-flavored breath wafted across her face, making her skin tighten longingly. "Actually, what I had in mind was the end of the story, where the prince wakes her up with a kiss."

He reached out and, grasping the back of her neck, gently tugged her toward him. Addy went willingly.

"If it was good enough for Sleeping Beauty, who am I to complain?"

"Who, indeed?" Joe murmured against her mouth a second before his lips closed over hers. Addy shuddered at the desire that coiled through her, and she opened her mouth beneath his onslaught. His tongue quickly took advantage and surged into her mouth, rubbing over the line of her teeth.

Much too soon for Addy's fevered senses, he withdrew and stared down into her dazed eyes. "It doesn't seem to be working," he said. "You still look out of it."

And would like to be even further out of it, Addy thought, finding it inconceivable that he didn't seem to realize the effect his kisses had on her. The only possibility that occurred to her was that he didn't find their kisses anywhere near as potent as she did. It was not a line of thought that she wanted to follow, so she ignored it.

"What brings you home so early?" Addy asked as he walked into the living room.

"This!" Joe waved a sheath of papers at her.

Addy took them. The first sentence had three "wherefores" and two "whereases." "What exactly does all this legalese amount to?"

"The culmination of a lifetime ambition!" Joe gloated. "I've finally got the bastard where I want him."

"If you had a mustache to twirl, we could cast you as Sir Jasper!" Worry made her voice sharp.

"Who?"

"You remember. The villain who went around evicting women and children from their run-down shacks."

Joe's lips tightened. "The run-down shack in this case is a twenty-two-room mansion."

Addy's mouth fell open in shock. It was even worse than she'd thought. "Do you mean to tell me that you actually hold the mortgage on his house, too?"

"Damn right I do," he muttered. "I've got it all. Edwards is going to pay."

"David doesn't owe you anything!" Addy yelled at him, as if the very strength of her voice could make him listen.

"Edwards got everything his father had to leave."

"Which didn't appear to be all that much. So now what? Do you intend to take those blasted foreclosure papers out to the cemetery and wave them around under Edwards's tombstone? Or maybe you could hold a séance and have a medium tell him that you finally won."

"His son will know," Joe insisted.

Addy nodded. "And he has to pay because he's Edwards's son. You're his son, too. What are you going to pay?"

"I've already paid!"

Addy stared at him in frustration. What could she say to

get through to him? To make him realize that his drive for revenge was far more likely to hurt him than David. All David stood to lose were things. Joe was compromising his integrity, his basic sense of decency and fair play.

"What about David himself?" she tried.

"Edwards."

"No! Not Edwards. David. Your brother, David." Addy struggled to make him see David as a person in his own right.

Joe glared at her. His face was set in hard lines, and his eyes burned with a fury that filled her with despair. "That's what this is all about, isn't it?" he growled. "David Edwards. You don't care about me. All you care about is that he not get hurt."

"No!" Addy responded to the underlying pain in his voice. Pain that she was sure he wasn't aware he'd revealed. "Why can't you see that—"

"Oh, I can see. Finally." Stiffly, he turned and stalked out of the cottage.

"What are you planning on doing with the rest of your life now that you've achieved all your ambitions?" Addy yelled after him. She slammed her door shut, wishing she could shut out her feeling of hopeless frustration as well.

Flinging herself down on the sofa, she wrapped her arms around her legs and rested her chin on her knees. Her old psychology professor had been right. You couldn't reason with a fanatic, and that's what Joe was on the subject of the Edwards family.

But revenge had a nasty way of rebounding. Usually on innocent bystanders. She sniffed as an unhappy tear trickled down her cheek. Such as herself. Joe had forced her into the position of defending his worst enemy, and he refused to believe that it wasn't for David's sake, but for his own.

As Joe would eventually find out. Destroying people came with a price tag, and sooner or later the bill would come due. There were a lot of people in this town who remembered David with pleasure and the Edwards family with loyalty. The old man might have been every bit as

bad as Joe claimed, but until his stroke he'd run a very
efficient company that had provided good, well-paying jobs
for a great many of the people. They were going to resent
what Joe was doing to David.

By foreclosing, Joe would never have a chance of finding
an accepted place in the town's social structure.

Addy's lower lip trembled. Joe would probably decide
to leave, and then she wouldn't even be able to see him
from a distance once in a while. The tears began to pour
harder as a vision of the empty years ahead engulfed her.
It wasn't fair, she thought fuzzily. Why did she have to fall
in love with a man who not only didn't want to love her,
but didn't intend to love any woman? Why couldn't she
have fallen in love with some nice, normal man who wasn't
obsessed with the past?

She rocked back and forth, trying to ease the pain burning deep inside her. When she'd so blithely started out to
find a husband, the worst that she'd thought would happen
would be that she wouldn't be successful. It had never occurred to her that looking for happiness might bring her the
greatest unhappiness she'd ever known. She leaned her
forehead against her knees and gave in to the despair well-
ing in her. Why shouldn't she cry? she thought miserably.
Her whole life had just come tumbling down around her
ears. Who had a better right?

"I already have a son. I don't need to acknowledge a
bastard like you." His father's scathing words surfaced out
of the depths of Joe's memories as he stalked across the
yard between Addy's cottage and his house. Shoving open
his front door, he slammed it behind him with enough force
to rattle the delicate stained glass in it. The violence didn't
help to dissipate the anger and hurt that were seething
through him.

Once again, someone preferred his half brother to him.
But this time it was worse. Far worse. He hadn't known
his father, and what little he had known he hadn't liked.
His father's rejection had filled him with a burning sense

of injustice and anger and a desire to get even. To somehow make Edwards pay for his callousness.

Stamping over to the antique liquor cabinet, he jerked out a crystal decanter of whiskey. He splashed some in a glass, as well as all over the exquisitely refinished wood, and swallowed the liquor in one gulp. It didn't do a thing to help numb the pain that seemed to be ripping him apart.

He refilled the glass to the brim and, wandering over to the sofa, dropped down onto it.

"Why?" The anguished word echoed around the room. After everything they'd shared, how could Addy defend that...that... Joe drained the rest of the whiskey and stared down into the empty glass as if seeking an answer in it. There was no enlightenment to be found there, so he dropped it onto the coffee table with a thump.

"She's only a woman. One of millions," he tried to tell himself. The problem was that he knew better. Addy wasn't one of millions. She was one in a million. And it wasn't just the sex. It was everything about her. The wholehearted way she went about things. Her determination. Her compassion. Her sense of humor. The way she laughed at him with her eyes. The way her soft lips quivered when she was trying not to laugh.

He shifted restlessly as his body began to react to his memories. The thought of never getting to kiss her again, of never having her listen to him tell her about his day, filled him with a sick feeling deep in his guts. Because he loved her. The truth exploded in his mind. He loved Adelaide Edson.

Leaning his head back against the sofa, he took several deep, sustaining breaths as a panicky feeling of having lost control filled him. He didn't want to be in love. Not with anyone. Being in love left you vulnerable. Look at what that much-vaunted emotion had done to his mother.

Joe stared blindly at the ceiling, unable to shut out the cool, incisive sound of Addy's voice telling him that his mother had chosen to drink. He tried to imagine Addy sinking into an alcoholic stupor and leaving her child to fend for itself, and failed completely. Addy would move away, get a job and set about building a life for that child.

That was one of the things that he liked about Addy. She was strong. Strong mentally and, with the exception of her strange blind spot about her weight, emotionally. She was a fighter. Like he was. The fact that she fought for other people while he'd had to fight for himself, didn't matter. What mattered was that they were very much alike.

He jackknifed to his feet and began to pace. He tried to force himself to think. It was hard. The knowledge that he was losing Addy kept muddling his thoughts.

One fact stood out. Addy was mad because he was about to get even with Edwards. So if he didn't carry out his revenge, then she wouldn't be mad, right? He frowned. Maybe, but even if she was no longer mad at him, that wouldn't mean that she loved him. Or would ever come to love him.

Addy wanted a family, he reminded himself. She wanted a husband and she wanted children. A shaft of longing pieced his gloomy thoughts. He wanted her children to be his. He wanted to be the man to sire them. He wanted to have Addy's children to raise and to love. Love as his mother had never loved him. He might not know anything about how a happy family operated, but he could learn from Addy.

He pressed his lips together in determination. All he had to do was to convince her to marry him. But he couldn't ask her now. Not while she was still so upset about Edwards. He'd have to convince her that he was no longer interested in revenge. Not that it was true. He'd still like to destroy Edwards. He just wanted Addy far more than he wanted revenge. Giving up his plans was a small price to pay for the chance of marrying Addy.

He'd tell Addy that he wasn't going to do it. He started toward the door and then stopped. Telling her might not convince her. It would be better to show her. He glanced up at the clock. Edwards was due here in less than an hour. He would ask Addy to come over at six, and then he'd tell

Edwards that he was going to give him an extension on the loan. That he'd extend it for as long as Edwards needed. Hell, Joe thought on a rising tide of optimism, if Addy would agree to marry him, Edwards could have the money and welcome to it.

Addy carefully added a little more makeup around her eyes, trying to hide the results of her bout of crying. It helped a little.

If only she knew why Joe had asked her to come over to the house. She very much feared that he was simply going to try to convince her that what he was doing to David was right. She sniffed unhappily. One thing was certain: he couldn't reason with her about his attitude because there was nothing reasonable about it. It was totally irrational.

Addy let herself out of the cottage and headed toward Joe's house, taking deep breaths to still her racing heart. She wanted to see him so much. No matter how wrong he was or how mad he was, she still wanted to see him.

She knocked on the front door and then jumped when it opened immediately. Eagerly, her eyes skimmed over Joe's taut features and her heart sank. He looked tense and determined. Very determined.

"What…" she began and then turned as she heard the sound of a car coming up the driveway. A black BMW. She peered through the windshield as it approached, shivering when she recognized David.

Joe had to have known that David was coming, she thought in dismay. It was simply too much of a coincidence otherwise. Which meant Joe wanted her here for this meeting. Why?

The obvious answer was not reassuring. Joe was stubborn enough to ask her to witness it just to show her that she couldn't influence him. Her heart sank as she watched David get out of his car.

"Good evening," David greeted them. "Your lawyer

asked me to meet you here at six, Mr. Barrington, but if this is a bad time…''

"No, this won't take long," Joe said and, stepping out of the doorway, motioned them both inside.

Addy trailed into the living room and perched gingerly on the edge of the sofa. She didn't want to be here. She didn't want to watch David being humiliated, and she most definitely didn't want to watch Joe doing it. But what could she do. Leave? Her gaze lingered on Joe's pale face. He might be wrong in what he was about to do, but it didn't make any difference about how she felt about him. She still loved him to distraction. She wanted to shield him somehow from the consequences of what he was going to do.

"Your lawyer mentioned that you had acquired the first loan I took out on the factory last winter, Mr. Barrington." David grimaced. "And since it's overdue and the grace period is past, I would imagine you want to know how I intend to pay for it?"

"You have the money?" Addy asked hopefully.

David snorted inelegantly. "Don't I wish. I not only don't have the money, I don't have the slightest shot of getting it. I guess it's foreclosure time. I won't fight you."

"It needn't come to that." Joe muttered the words as if he were having trouble articulating them.

"You mean declare bankruptcy?" David said. "I thought of that, but to do it, I have to show some plan for getting out of my financial difficulties. And to be frank, the court probably wouldn't accept my hope of winning the lottery as adequate security."

Joe waved his hand impatiently as if he wanted to get the whole thing over with. "I'll hold the loans as long as you need."

Addy's mouth dropped open, and she stared at Joe unable to believe her ears. He'd actually done it. He'd changed his mind because she had asked him to. A warm feeling of euphoria began to bubble through her. Joe might not love her, but he liked her enough to give up plans he'd made long ago. It was a start.

She beamed at him when what she wanted to do was to throw her arms around him and kiss him. To slip her hand beneath his shirt and rub her palm over the deliciously ticklish hair on his chest. She wanted to—

"...so sure that's a good idea," David's voice interrupted her thoughts, and she turned to him in confusion.

"Not that I don't appreciate your offer, Mr. Barrington, but the plain fact of the matter is that I have neither the basic business sense nor the experience to run a company. Quite frankly, I'm in way over my head."

"But you could learn," Addy said, annoyed at David. Here Joe was making a grand gesture, the scope of which David couldn't begin to understand, and David was refusing it.

David sighed. "So my father used to claim. I didn't believe it then, and I don't now. You either have the flair for business like my father and Mr. Barrington do or you don't. I don't."

Addy noticed Joe's wince at having his name coupled with Andrew Edwards's and hurried to divert David before he began to wonder about Joe's reaction. "But if you weren't interested in business, why did you come back from California and try to run the factory?"

"Loyalty," David said promptly. "Most of the employees have been there for decades. I felt I had to make an effort to save their jobs."

Addy noticed the expression on Joe's face and gave him a warning glance. If he said one word about noblesse oblige, she'd thump him. To her relief he didn't.

David shrugged. "Unfortunately, good intentions simply aren't enough. It has been a very salutary experience. I am considered a very good English literature professor, but those skills didn't carry over into the business world. No, I really think that the best thing to do would be to let you take over the company, Mr. Barrington. That way the employees will still have jobs, and I can go back to teaching with a clear conscience."

Joe stared at him as if trying to assimilate what had been

said. He was obviously having a difficult time of it, and Addy's heart swelled with love for him.

"Um, I see," Joe finally said. "Well, the factory is worth more than the mortgages on it. How about if I sign over the mortgage on your house in exchange?"

Addy blinked, knowing how much Joe had wanted that house. To him it was the symbol of everything that he had been denied as a child. When he made a gesture, he didn't fool around.

"Thank you." David shook Joe's hand. "That offer I won't refuse. I intend to put it on the market immediately."

"You're going to sell it?" Joe sounded shocked.

"As soon as possible. I always hated that place." He sighed. "It was never a home. It was simply the arena my parents picked to stage their fights. Well, I won't keep you any longer. I want to call my lawyer and tell him what we've decided. It was nice seeing you again, Addy. I hope we have a chance to have dinner before I go back to California."

Addy nodded vaguely as he left.

The sound of the front door closing behind David seemed to jar Joe out of his daze, and he turned to Addy in confusion. "He doesn't want the factory. He doesn't even want the damn house!"

Addy tried to swallow the giggle that bubbled up and found that she couldn't contain it. It burst loose and echoed around the room.

Joe stared at her in impotent frustration. Somewhere, somehow, he'd completely lost control of the situation. "What's so damn funny?"

"You, me, David, life. And I'm not even sure if I should be laughing or crying." She made a valiant effort to contain her mirth. "It all seems so ironic. All these years you've schemed to take away his inheritance, and he couldn't wait to get rid of it."

Joe ran his fingers around the back of his neck. "It was a bit of a shock," he conceded.

"But it was a grand gesture." Addy smiled mistily at

him. "I'm very proud of you. It couldn't have been easy to give up your plans for revenge like that."

He shrugged. "It was surprisingly easy, considering the alterative. Addy... I... This harebrained idea you have about finding a husband..."

Addy watched him nervously, fearful of what he was about to say. Was he going to tell her that he'd had enough and wouldn't help her anymore? She took a deep breath and held it, hoping to contain the pain she could see coming.

"If you want a husband, I think you ought to marry me," he finally blurted out.

Addy blinked, wondering if she'd really heard what she thought she'd heard. Had Joe actually proposed to her? The buzzing in her ears reminded her that she wasn't breathing, and she hastily took a breath.

"You do?" she whispered.

"Damn right I do! At least, I love you. I know I'm not exactly what you would have chosen in a husband, but—"

"Ha! That just goes to show what you know. You are the perfect husband."

"I am?" He looked uncertainly at her.

"Perfect," she repeated. "You're kind and intelligent and sexy as all get out and I love you to distraction."

To her surprise, Joe grabbed her, pulling her up against him in a crushing embrace.

"What are you doing?" she asked, not really caring. It was enough to be so close to him

"A good businessman always knows when to talk and when to take action, and this is definitely a time for action."

Addy smiled seductively at him. "I'm always willing to be guided by an expert," she murmured against his mouth.

*　*　*　*　*

IN CELEBRATION OF MOTHER'S DAY, JOIN
SILHOUETTE THIS MAY AS WE BRING YOU

a funny thing
HAPPENED ON THE WAY TO THE
DELIVERY ROOM

THESE THREE STORIES, CELEBRATING THE
LIGHTER SIDE OF MOTHERHOOD, ARE
WRITTEN BY YOUR FAVORITE AUTHORS:

KASEY MICHAELS
KATHLEEN EAGLE
EMILIE RICHARDS

When three couples make the trip to the delivery
room, they get more than their own bundles of
joy…they get the promise of love!

Available this May,
wherever Silhouette books are sold.

Take 4 bestselling love stories FREE

Plus get a FREE surprise gift!

Special Limited-time Offer

Mail to Silhouette Reader Service™

3010 Walden Avenue
P.O. Box 1867
Buffalo, N.Y. 14240-1867

YES! Please send me 4 free Silhouette Desire® novels and my free surprise gift. Then send me 6 brand-new novels every month, which I will receive months before they appear in bookstores. Bill me at the low price of $2.90 each plus 25¢ delivery and applicable sales tax, if any.* That's the complete price and a savings of over 10% off the cover prices—quite a bargain! I understand that accepting the books and gift places me under no obligation ever to buy any books. I can always return a shipment and cancel at any time. Even if I never buy another book from Silhouette, the 4 free books and the surprise gift are mine to keep forever.

225 BPA A3UU

Name	(PLEASE PRINT)	
Address	Apt. No.	
City	State	Zip

This offer is limited to one order per household and not valid to present Silhouette Desire® subscribers. *Terms and prices are subject to change without notice.
Sales tax applicable in N.Y.

UDES-696

©1990 Harlequin Enterprises Limited

As seen on TV!
Free Gift Offer

With a Free Gift proof-of-purchase from any Silhouette® book,
you can receive a beautiful cubic zirconia pendant.

This gorgeous marquise-shaped stone is a genuine cubic
zirconia—accented by an 18" gold tone necklace.

(Approximate retail value $19.95)

Send for yours today...
compliments of ▼ *Silhouette*®
TM

To receive your free gift, a cubic zirconia pendant, send us one original proof-of-
purchase, photocopies not accepted, from the back of any Silhouette Romance™,
Silhouette Desire®, Silhouette Special Edition®, Silhouette Intimate Moments®
or Silhouette Yours Truly™ title available in February, March and April at your favorite
retail outlet, together with the Free Gift Certificate, plus a check or money order for
$1.65 U.S./$2.15 CAN. (do not send cash) to cover postage and handling, payable
to Silhouette Free Gift Offer. We will send you the specified gift. Allow 6 to 8 weeks for
delivery. Offer good until April 30, 1997 or while quantities last. Offer valid in the
U.S. and Canada only.

Free Gift Certificate

Name: _____

Address: _____

City: _____ State/Province: _____ Zip/Postal Code: _____

Mail this certificate, one proof-of-purchase and a check or money order for postage
and handling to: SILHOUETTE FREE GIFT OFFER 1997. In the U.S.: 3010 Walden
Avenue, P.O. Box 9077, Buffalo NY 14269-9077. In Canada: P.O. Box 613, Fort Erie,
Ontario L2Z 5X3.

FREE GIFT OFFER   084-KFD
ONE PROOF-OF-PURCHASE
To collect your fabulous FREE GIFT, a cubic zirconia pendant, you must include this
original proof-of-purchase for each gift with the properly completed Free Gift Certificate.

084-KFD

In April 1997
Bestselling Author

DALLAS SCHULZE

takes her Family Circle series to new heights with

TESSA'S CHILD

In April 1997 Dallas Schulze brings readers a
brand-new, longer, out-of-series title featuring the
characters from her popular Family Circle miniseries.

When rancher Keefe Walker found Tessa Wyndham he
knew that she needed a man's protection—she was
pregnant, alone and on the run from a heartless past.
Keefe was also hiding from a dark past...but in one
overwhelming moment he and Tessa forged a family
bond that could never be broken.

Available in April wherever books are sold.

You're About to Become a *Privileged Woman*

Reap the rewards of fabulous free gifts and benefits with proofs-of-purchase from Silhouette and Harlequin books

Pages & Privileges™

It's our way of thanking you for buying our books at your favorite retail stores.

PROOF OF PURCHASE
SD-PP23
Offer expires March 31, 1997

Pages & Privileges™

Harlequin and Silhouette—
the most privileged readers in the world!

For more information about Harlequin and Silhouette's PAGES & PRIVILEGES program call the Pages & Privileges Benefits Desk: 1-503-794-2499

Silhouette®

SD-PP23